Jed Dey and his father, a dealer in precious stones, left New York for the Far East in search of rare gold. But when seven months pass with no word from the expedition, Will Detroit, Jed's closest friend, abandons the glamorous whirl of turn-of-the-century New York society to lead a search party into the treacherous, snow-covered mountains of Tibet.

In a monastery hidden high in the rugged Himalayas, Will finds his friend utterly transformed and is forced to accept the shocking truth . . .

Jed does not want to be rescued.

LAND OF PRECIOUS SNOW

THADDEUS TULEJA

AVON
PUBLISHERS OF BARD, CAMELOT AND DISCUS BOOKS

AVON BOOKS
A division of
The Hearst Corporation
959 Eighth Avenue
New York, New York 10019

First Avon Printing, February, 1980

AVON TRADEMARK REG. U.S. PAT. OFF. AND IN
OTHER COUNTRIES, MARCA REGISTRADA,
HECHO EN U.S.A.

Printed in the U.S.A.

For the Past

CONTENTS

Who knows Spiritual Consciousness passes beyond death and enters Immortality.

—*Isopanishad*

CHAPTER 1

THE AVENUE

King Cane's fault, all of it.

Had the sugar tycoon been content to decorate his mansion with good American workmanship instead of a sybarite's hoard of Oriental baubles, John Pierre might never have been brought into his orbit, Jennifer would never have met his bohemian son, and there would be no talk of an expedition.

William Detroit shifted his considerable bulk irritably in the leather chair and whipped the tip of a slender cigar toward an ormolu ashstand to his right. A tall, stooping butler in a navy waistcoat scooped it into a long-handled brass dustpan before it had a chance to ravage the parquet floor.

"I'm sorry, Walter. There I go again. Bring me another?"

The resonant voice carried a hint of apology, as if Detroit, aware of the toll the cognac was taking on his body, sought to mitigate its effects by ingratiation. The servant accepted the glass with a nod. "The same again, sir?"

Detroit's large head bobbed once and he closed his eyes, allowing the echo of heels through the marble foyer to divert his attention for a moment from the matter at hand. Fleshy hands gnarled the *World* in his lap, and he screwed down his features into a wince of distaste. "Bad business," he muttered.

The man was still shy of half a century, and in spite of Walter's silent disapproval of his fondness for grapes and tobacco, he could hardly be called epicurean. His tastes, compared to those of most of his acquaintances, were modest, and he had scant patience for those of his set whose daily constitutionals were a matter of stepping from curb to trolley and back again. For the past twenty-five years only a particularly enervating bout with the flu, back in the bristling winter of 1882, had kept him from, each day at exactly two PM, pushing open the gleaming glass doors of the building on 43rd Street and beginning a brisk stride home to the corner of 71st and Fifth.

In his youth he had been a more than adequate sportsman. At Yale he had rowed single scull, and for many a summer after his graduation in the last year of the war, the Newport yachting set had welcomed his as coxswain in the annual contests between the Cambridge and New Haven contingents of the new money's most hallowed spa. Since entering legal service, however, the sedentary claims of an attorney's life had cut severely into his regimen, and in recent years, he was ashamed to acknowledge, walking was the sole exercise left him.

As a result, he did not take it lightly. He cherished his daily constitutional. It took him half an hour to clip from the club to his modest palace on 71st Street; in good weather, with the sun darting from window to high window around the Plaza, no Wordsworthian vision could have tempted him away from the delights of this stroll.

Middle age, however, had in spite of his efforts endowed him with a small double chin and a considerable paunch. As he was a large man to begin with, this modest corpulence, combined with his slumping position in the armchair and the pursing disapproval of his face, served to render his appearance, at this moment in the afternoon light of the Century Club's quiet parlor, somewhat porcine. Dissonant news often had this effect on him.

He slapped the paper hard on his thigh and returned to the story that had put him in ill humor. The writing was typical of the new "yellow" journalism that was beginning to insinuate itself into even the more respectable dailies.

"SUGAR DUKE" TO SPONSOR FAR EAST SEARCH
Trust's Attorney Mounts Expedition to Find Daughter's Fiance, Missing a Year

The big head shook sadly. Count on the *World* to compound its usual indelicacy with a string of inaccuracies even before the story began. His nostrils flared stiffly as he attacked the story for the third time that day.

Mr. William P. Detroit, Sr. of 2 East 71st Street was said to be planning a Far Eastern expedition to search for his fellow millionaire and friend John Pierre Dey and Dey's 20-year-old son Jethro, who left New York over a year ago and have not been heard from since last July.

The elder Dey, a dealer in precious stones, was hired in the spring of last year by sugar tycoon Horace Holmohr to undertake a tour of the Far East to purchase jewels and other items for the new Holmohr mansion at 14 East 66th Street. Young Mr. Dey, then in his junior year at Harvard, was to accompany his father as far

13

as Calcutta and return to the United States in time for the 1896 fall term.

However, nothing was heard from the two between their departure in March and last July, when a letter to Mr. Detroit, posted in Calcutta, informed the concerned members of Millionaires' Row that young Jethro would not be back on schedule and that father and son were about to embark on a journey "north to Tibet."

For the past seven months no word has reached New York of the whereabouts of the two travelers.

Mr. Detroit—unofficially known on the rolls of Society as the "Sugar Duke"—is Mr. Holmohr's personal legal counsel. He was recently subpoenaed along with his employer by a Senate antitrust subcommittee as part of its investigation of abuses of corporate power within the Sugar Trust. That investigation, in which the Holmohr interests are suspected of having watered stock, bribed legislators, and manipulated tariff reform procedures, is still pending.

As a result, Mr. Detroit may not be permitted to leave the country at this time, and there is speculation that, if a search expedition is formed, it will be headed by his son, William, Jr., a former classmate of the Dey boy and reportedly his closest friend.

Reached at the Yale Club yesterday, the younger Mr. Detroit expressed the opinion that "foreign elements" had likely kidnapped the two Deys in hopes of ransom, although no communication from the suspected villains has yet been received. "All I know," he concluded, "is that we're going to do our utmost to get Jed and Uncle John back safe."

Mr. Detroit is married to the former Lavinia Phelps Windsor of Philadelphia. Their second child, Jennifer, 19, is said to be "unofficially betrothed" to young Dey, but neither she nor her parents could be reached for comment.

Should an expedition in fact be mounted, reliable estimates are that it will cost at least $5,000 in Holmohr and Detroit money.

Detroit rattled the paper shut and downed his drink. He coughed once, hard, as if to expel the foulness of the narrative, and rose from the chair. He straightened a broad silk tie, closed the front of his jacket, and reached his arms back to where the percipient Walter was already holding open a coat. He slipped his arms into the camel sleeves and took a tall felt hat from the servant's hands. "Walter?" he mused.

"Sir?"

"Is this hat ridiculous?"

"Must of cost a pretty penny, sir."

"A man in my position, Walter, doesn't worry about pennies. He worries about appearance. What do you think, man?" He stuffed the hat on top of his head. "Do I look ridiculous?"

The servant squeezed his eyes appraisingly. "I'm sure I wouldn't know if a gentleman's hat was ridiculous or not, sir. Seems a bit topheavy, if you know what I mean."

Detroit finished buttoning up his coat and surveyed the butler kindly. Sandy brows knit together momentarily, and then the broad face brightened with the recognition of a private and wonderful absurdity. A short laugh burst from the big man's frame and the servant's neck straightened as he tried to determine whether he was being applauded or mocked.

He was still laughing as he pushed through the glass doors into the winter sunshine of 43rd Street.

"Topheavy! Oh, good, Walter, very good! Very good, indeed."

The thirty-odd years since the end of the Civil War had seen not only the establishment of most of the young nation's major fortunes, but dissension and enmity as well. For every Horace Holmohr, ensconced in Byzantine glory on Fifth Avenue, a thousand souls toiled in the sweatshops south of Houston Street, toiled ten years for what he might spend on a single season's fancy. For every gentleman's club, softlit with roses and cognac, there were a thousand tenement flats where the amenities were limited to cold water, papered windows, and stale beer. For every cotillion charted carefully past the shoals of *gaucherie* by matrons of the new money, there were a thousand flophouses and airshaft bunkers and curbstone gambling dens swelling with the human refuse of this century of splendor—that vast ragtallion horde to whom the blessings of liberty had been so far denied. New York City in 1897—one year after populism had gone down feebly waving the sententious banner of William Jennings Bryan—was a city cut in two.

William Detroit was not unaware of this. True, as a marginal member of New York's "400"—the number of fortunate souls, it was said, who could, without inconvenience, be accommodated in Mrs. William Astor's new ballroom—he had been somewhat isolated from the harsher realities of what the outraged journalist Jacob Riis called "how the other half lives." But as attorney to one of the monarchs of the American sugar trade, it was his business to be aware of the latest designs of unionists, anarchists, and reformers; as a result, he had kept reasonably abreast of the state of affairs in Manhattan's troubled streets. If it could not be said that he actually trod the verminous parts of town himself, still he was well and constantly acquainted—unlike many of his class—with the curious designs of bolsheviks, suffragettes, Free Silver supporters, and those of like ilk.

His employer had entrusted him with the management of the legal affairs of one of the major commercial enterprises of the nation, and for nearly a decade William Detroit had been diligent in honoring that trust. Dutifully he had denounced the 1886 Homestead Strike and the Pullman debacle of three years ago. His sonorous assurances to the stockholders that the dislocations of 1893 ("This was the fault of the Sherman Act!" he intoned) would not extend to the sugar industry were received with the moist-eyed gratitude of the newly prosperous. Throughout the bitter 1896 campaign, he railed against the fulminations of the scarlet spoilers who, he had no doubt, had been sent from Germany to unsettle the recent happiness of this great land. His mouth, no less than his acute legal eye, was ever at the company's service. His efforts had earned him the respect of his peers, the indulgence of the 400, and the not entirely happy sobriquet of "Sugar Duke."

William Detroit, then, by the last decade of an exceedingly active century, had arrived. He could not count himself among the hypereans Morgan, Carnegie, and Gould. Nor could he pretend full membership in the 400; of that august company he remained still an occasional guest. Yet he had not done badly. His holdings were in the tens of millions; his modest mansion sat on the Avenue only five blocks north of Holmohr's own; he possessed an adoring and attractive wife, two sturdy children, a cottage at fashionable Newport, a *pied-á-terre* in Paris, an unostentatious number of servants, membership in the redoubtable Stanford White's own club, and no less than a dozen of the finest Arabian stallions this side of Mecca. Only last year he had endowed a small library. Until a month ago, he had been accustomed to spend his afternoons at the club looking forward with patrician stoicism to the twilight of his years and the opening of a second hundred years of splendor.

The new year, true, had been hard. Scarcely had the Christmas tree been carted away when the ten-year-old Interstate Commerce Commission, invoking the new Sherman Antitrust Act, had called the attorney and his employer to Washington (that lurid provincial town!) to answer charges made by a group of disgruntled unionists that they had, under the aegis of the Sugar Trust, misused public funds.

Public funds! As if the public had the faintest idea of how to run an industry!

Well, the investigation had concluded nothing as yet, and Detroit could continue to endure their taunts with the good grace of a man whose estimation of the popular press oscillated, depending on the acerbity of the copy, between amused indulgence and disdain.

This new aggravation, however . . . this one irked him.

Tibet! No one—not even the Van Damms, who had been everywhere—went to Tibet. It was white space on the map. A secret satisfaction enhanced his antipathy for the project: had not John and the boy got pretty much what they deserved? India, by dammit, was bad enough; only a family as eccentric as the Deys would have conceived the notion of Tibet in the first place. Did that mean that Detroit was obliged to send his only son (no matter how eager the fool was to go) down that unbeaten track after them?

Damn Holmohr, anyway! A year ago this month it had been. They had gathered in his palace on 66th to celebrate the betrothal of his niece to the scion of a Chicago meatpacking family. Detroit recalled the occasion especially well because it was the first time since Janet's

18

death that the father and son had ventured out socially: they were still wearing crepe that night.

With them was a tall Levantine who, Detroit supposed, could be said to be the root of all this trouble. Haji something-or-other. An Arab, anyway. On his vest he wore a flat disc of white gold, worked intricately with Oriental ideograms. He came, he said, from a line of merchants who had been passing this curious and— Detroit had to admit—quite beautiful item from generation to generation since before the time of the Crusades. It was as a result of these centuries of handling worn to a smooth luster.

The King of Cane had seen it straight off, and had to have it. No, protested the Arab, it was not for sale. Figures flew and multiplied. Somewhere around $50,000 had come Holmohr's desperate plea: "At any price. I insist." But it was still no go. The Arab assured the tycoon that his store of wares—which could, incidentally, be inspected at the shop of Monsieur Dey— contained many pieces of far greater beauty than this humble medallion. The sugar king was welcome to take his pick of them without charge.

Holmohr would have none of it. Years of collecting had sharpened his eye and pampered his taste. He could not be persuaded to give up his designs on the piece because, as he explained to the company, "It ain't no common bauble."

John Pierre's expert opinion was solicited and given. Yes, the piece was fine and rare. The workmanship was unexceptional, but the quality of the gold itself was extraordinary. Only once or twice before—during his youthful travels with his father—had he seen anything like it. That dull, whitish sheen was peculiar to gold refined only in the central Asian mountains, and few examples had ever found their way beyond the subcontinent. He had, in fact, never before seen this kind of gold in the West, and could well understand why their guest was reluctant to part with it.

"Well, then," interrupted Holmohr, "you'd not have another piece like it in your stock?"

The Arab attempting conciliation, spoke with deference. "Not of this particular gold, sir. However, I do have—"

"No!" The sugar king ran a hand through white hair and turned to Dey. "Where'd you say they do this work?"

"The Himalayas. North of India. Tibet, Nepal."

"Go there, then. Get me one. Get several. I want that gold."

And that was it. A merchant's whim, a nod to the one man whose taste he trusted as firmly as his own, and the affair was settled. Within a month father and son had embarked, amid the tears and fond farewells of the Detroit brood, for Paris, thence to make the arduous journey to Istanbul, Calcutta, Kathmandu—and the Himalayas.

At first Detroit had welcomed the idea. At the least the journey would take six months: plenty of time for Jenny to get over her infatuation for the young bohemian, plenty of time, too, for John and Jed (for he was not unmindful of their feelings) to get over the still raw wound of Janet's death. Without stint he had agreed to Jenny's demand that, should they not return within a year, the Detroit fortune would be pressed into the service of finding them. Surely by May, the father reasoned, the girl would have put him behind her and immersed herself in the flurry of the season.

He had not, however, counted on either the doggedness of youthful ardor or the capriciousness of the mails. For three months Jed wrote her regularly, and he too received the occasional mailgram from John, informing him that Paris had proved a dead end, Istanbul was no good, Calcutta had beggers but no gold—until, late in September, Jennifer had received the last note. Posted from Calcutta in July, it was a model of tantalizing brevity.

NO LUCK HERE. NORTH TO TIBET. LOVE.
JED.

There followed an anxious five months, and then the storm broke. Jennifer could wait no longer, she accused her father of welshing on his word, young Will was eager to taste adventure, Holmohr was getting worried about his delegate, and, in fact, Detroit himself was more than a little concerned for his friend. Last week he had made the error of broaching the mere possibility of an expedition at a pointedly private family dinner, and three days later Will had let the cat out. The result was the lubricious tale in today's *World*.

Detroit pulled up the foxfur collar of his coat and paused on the corner of 46th Street. He breathed the brisk February air and, deciding to forego inspection of the new Brooks line until later in the week, continued walking north. North, he snorted, to Tibet, reflecting how his affection for John Pierre had never fully extended—in spite of his children's infatuation—to the son.

He supposed he should have known: the father himself was no model of regularity.

The Deys, in fact, had always been peculiar. The clan's patriarch, one Count Isarn de Dei, had in the First Crusade been a Grand Master of the Ordre de Seigneurs Teutonique—an organization, as John Pierre used to say with wry chagrin, whose crusading zeal had had at least as much to do with plunder as with piety. The Count's descendants remained prosperous and devoted to Church and country for six centuries. Then, in

1685, when the revocation of the Edict of Nantes forced thousands of Protestants to flee France for sanctuary in England and the Low Countries, the Catholic Deys—for reasons philosophical or mercenary none could say—joined the exodus, becoming merchants among the Dutch. It was not until after the 1789 Revolution that any of them returned: it was with the birth in French Canada of John Pierre's father, that irascible old prospector Jean-Louis, that the American chapters of the Dey history had begun.

A finger of sour nostalgia hooked Detroit's brain. He recalled the day, half a lifetime ago, that the old man had arrived on the Avenue with mud on his boots and twelve steamer trunks in tow. John Pierre had been in his teens then, and yet in spite of his youth and his father's archly cavalier attitude toward Dame Etiquette, he had been sized up at a glance as among the most eligible and engaging new additions to Millionaires' Row. Wiry, witty, and dark, he moved among the bright lights of Society like some exotic *bête noire* come to tease vinuousness out of its pretentions and announce to all the world that even here, among the nation's most extraordinarily inbred social set, a man could survive on little more than charm.

While his father immured himself in a small townhouse on Madison Avenue (wags said it might as well have been the West Side), refusing dinner invitations that others would have pawned children to accept, the son lilted, all magic and French promise, through a hundred balls a season. He had a graciousness and a humor that made him friends even among rivals, and by the winter of 1874 no one on the Avenue was surprised to read in the society column that the young man, then only twenty-three, had won the heart and hand of the reserved Bostonian beauty Janet Lansing.

It was quite a step up from the gold fields, thought

Detroit. He smiled, thinking of the first time he had seen the old man, with his crushed hat, burrs in his beard, and raving in his eye. And surrounded by twelve trunks full of God knew how many kings' ransoms.

Jean-Louis Armand Dey, as he liked to call himself then, was perhaps fifty when he arrived in New York. He had lived until 1889, Detroit recalled, but he was fifty when he came with the trunks. That must have been around 1870, perhaps a little earlier.

He spoke a grating *patois* of Provincial French, mountain slang, and—if the legend be true—an Indian tongue from somewhere just east of the Rockies. Gruff, unshaven, and rude to a fine degree, he dressed, drank, and swore like a mountain man. No brush had touched his boots, no comb his head, and there was not a man or woman among the lights of the Avenue who could, until at least a month had passed, make out a word he said. It was generally assumed this incomprehensibility was intended.

The two, it was known, had traveled. Out of the pieces of the legend, this chronology: John Pierre had been born around midcentury in the gold fields. His mother was unknown; most assumed it was from her that the father and son had acquired their facility in heathen tongues. It was said she died shortly after the birth of the baby, and that the two grieving survivors then undertook to escape her memory by encircling the globe. The flight brought them first to Central America, then by steamer to China, India, and Japan, where the former prospector augmented his knowledge of the precious things of the earth by purchasing, ultimately, twelve trunks full of jade, amber, turquoise, beryl, and silver. Apparently the father had eked something out of the fields, for he paid for everything with gold.

Around 1860, when John Pierre was ten, the two reached Paris. For the next decade they roved the winding streets of the Quartier Latin, a curious pair amid the splendor of the city of light. Baron Haussman's plan was just then being implemented, and for the burgeoning middle class for whom that classical revival was conducted, Dey père et fils provided a steady supply of decorative Orientalia. By 1870 Jean-Louis had established himself as second only to Tiffany as a purveyor of arcane decor to the new *beau monde*.

But not for long. La Commune changed everything. As Paris was rudely transformed in 1871 and the riches of his clients began to be appropriated by the revolutionaries, Jean-Louis took his son out of the Sorbonne and rushed to Le Havre. There, grumbling and spitting tobacco juice, the father supervised the loading of his glittering stock onto yet another steamer, and for the last time bid adieu to la belle France.

Even these bare facts of the history were enough to convince Detroit that the Deys were bound to be strange. Although he was among the first to welcome them to New York (in spite of his antipathy to rebellious foreign notions, he retained a vestigial affection for his countrymen) and although he and John Pierre had become quick if not deep friends, he could not but wonder at what recesses of instability there lay within a mind that had spent its formative years among wild Indians, Chinamen, and Parisians.

They got along. The last quarter century had passed amiably enough. In 1874 John Pierre had married Janet; a year later Detroit was married himself. He and Dey, due to their mutual association with King Cane—he as legal, John Pierre as artistic, adviser— were much thrown together. They learned to accept temperamental differences; grew fond of argument, cognac, and chess; settled into a placid tolerance of each other's idiosyncracies; and had become, by the time the elder Dey was ready to pass on the business in 1886, daily companions.

They lunched together at the Century, where the talk was of stock prices and war. Dey's politics irked Detroit considerably: from anyone but an undisputed member of his own set, he would have dismissed them as rabid nonsense. When the Haymarket anarchists were executed in 1886, Detroit was astounded to hear his friend defend their right to a "fair" trial; what trial had they given the murdered policemen? He also felt the United States ought not to have deprived the native aborigines of their land, ought not to be involved in Panama, ought not to protect its own industries by tariff . . . and so on.

On the Sherman Act Dey was understandably reticent. It would not do to have Holmohr, irked by a thoughtless word, shift his considerable patronage to Tiffany; and John was no fool. But he was raucous indeed on the free trade issue, and had antagonized more than one sugar executive by suggesting that the trust's support of high tariffs was self-serving.

Janet had been no better. Suffragette at eighteen, she had squandered more than a little of her father's money on this woman Addams in Chicago, and there had been talk, in 1892, that certain clandestine gifts to Henry George's single-tax campaign had come from her drawing room in the house on 82nd Street.

Detroit liked things simple. His politics like his clothes were clean, straight, without subtlety. It was obvious to him that the only conscionable vote for a man of his position was Republican; that wealth was a gift of hard work and penury the reward of sloth; that the great fortunes amassed since the War could survive only if men of his caliber banded together against the growing numbers of bomb-happy sentimentalists; that for the land he loved, just now burgeoning into the crest of a new century, there were but two choices: the fulfillment of her manifest destiny, or decline.

None of this, he chafed, was clear to John Pierre's son. The mother's profligate social sympathies, the father's contentious wit, had combined to produce a sensibility both tender and acute—a sensibility, Detroit recriminated, perfectly ripe for plucking by the "progressive" forces who, under the control of Charles Eliot Norton, now ruled Harvard University. The school that had educated presidents was now producing the likes of the Negro radical W.E.B. DuBois, the Jew freethinker Santayana, and Jed's own eccentric tutor, that ranting oddfellow Yarrowville.

Detroit had warned Janet and John about the place, had offered to write a recommendation to his own alma mater, where education still came from the great books of the West; they had dismissed him with that indulgent half-smile which, through 20 years of marriage, had gradually come to assume between them the questionable dignity of mutual complicity.

So Jed had gone to Harvard and had come back, as Detroit had predicted, confused, unsettled, and proud. To his father's political inconsistency he added an ingenuousness all his own; by the first Thanksgiving break he had begun to dabble in everything from Oriental mysticism to poetry. If he could be said to have a philosophy at all, it was a purely negative one, resting on an unquestioning hostility to everything his New York background had taught him to revere. He was no longer Jethro Dey, heir to one of the minor American fortunes; fed by Eliot's company, he had become Jed Dey, philosophe, knight errant, quack.

The nonsense he had talked that first vacation! Spouting bits of the "Gita" and the Transcendentalists, chewing vegetables, boasting that next to Will, Jr., his best friend was that anarchist Yarrowville. Was it any wonder he had ended up in Tibet?

And this was the young man whom his daughter, no less than his son, had pledged him to recover.

What she saw in him Detroit could not fathom. "The quality of his doubt is really wonderful, Father," she had said once in his defense. Whatever that might mean. No, youthful infatuation was not a subject on which he could boast much competence. Jennifer had quite unseated him last week when he had dared to suggest that she might do well to begin considering alternatives to Jed's return.

"You don't mean, Father," she had eyed him acidly, "that you would consider leaving them there?"

Father had shifted, grumbled in silence, assured her that of course he meant no such thing. Yes, surely there would be an expedition, but only wait a month or two more.

"With Jed in God knows what black hole! He may be dead already! We've a duty here. To friendship, if nothing else."

And on until Detroit had no recourse. There was nothing for it but to agree to a search and hope that the time spent in Paris and London—at the height of the season, he mused—would deflect some of this adolescent desperation into a more productive mode, and that Jenny, whom he could not deny, might with time and circumstance soften her demands.

Not that Detroit was averse to getting them back. Twenty years of acquaintance with the father had made him fully responsive to the dictates of friendship. He knew that, whatever the attractions of keeping the son away from his children, Jennifer was right about duty. And Detroit had never been one to shirk duty.

So, he supposed: Tibet.

*   *   *

She was waiting for him on the near corner of 57th, notebook in hand and hair protruding on all sides from what a kind fashion writer had once called a "serviceable" bonnet. Her eyes had keyed him down two blocks away. Detroit knew there was nothing for it but to hold brief court with her, trusting that his hold on the courtesies would prevent his saying anything that might be used to his disadvantage in tomorrow's edition. As he crossed 56th Street he put on a dignified smile and cursed himself silently for not making the swing at 44th Street to check out Brooks. Lavinia would be justifiably remonstrant this evening. He regretted his regularity.

"Good afternoon, Mr. Detroit. Got a minute?"

"Good afternoon, Miss Carew." He resented doffing his hat to her, but custom dictated no less, and he did so thoughtlessly. "Are you by any chance responsible for the amusing tidbit of misinformation in today's *World?*"

"Misinformation, is it?" Her pencil poised. "Perhaps you would be so kind as to enlighten me."

Detroit affected the paternal gentleness one might adopt for a child having difficulty with sums.

"First, my daughter is not engaged—unofficially or otherwise—to Jethro Dey. Second, the last correspondence from Mr. Dey was in September, not July. Third, may I say it was kind of you, after having excoriated my employer and myself for everything short of tyranny, to include the afterthought that the investigation (in which, may I remind you, we are both fully cooperating) is still pending: in fact not a shred of evidence has suggested that any of the charges are well founded. Fourth, I would appreciate it greatly if you would confine the mention of my wife's and daughter's names to the society column, where a lady's appearance is not unseemly. And fifth, I cannot imagine how a young

woman who earns—shall I guess, $1000 per annum?—
can be in a position to estimate the expense of a project
as extraordinary as an expedition—which, may I remind you, is anything but a foregone conclusion. Have
you got that all?"

Libby Carew stopped writing to smile broadly. "It
does amaze me, Mr. Detroit, how a man of your obvious articulateness can be so ingeniously obtuse to
the truly pressing matters of the day. Do you suppose
my readers are interested in measuring pennies with
you? Can it possibly matter to a journeyman making
$800 per annum whether you are about to spend $5000
or $50,000 on this global junket? I confess the $5000
figure is my own speculation, but unless you disclaim
it, it shall stand in tomorrow's edition. As for your
other quibbles: I am not in the least interested in
whether your women appear in the society column, the
front page, or the commodities advertisements. The
mention of them at all was a concession to my editor,
who is fond of what he calls 'human interest.' I myself
would prefer to use my limited space in getting behind
this investigation—the charges which, may I remind
you, proceed neither from myself nor from my paper,
but from our common government. Do I take it you
deny their substance?"

She was still smiling broadly. Detroit quickened his
pace, not so much to lose her as to aggravate her, and
grunted. "I do, Madam."

"I am not your madam, sir. I am a woman, attempting to present facts to my readers on an annual salary
—if this will satisfy your patrician curiosity—amount-
ing approximately to what your employer spends in that
time on ice cream. Do you think there will be a war in
Cuba?"

The abruptness of the transition jolted him only for a

moment. "War, Miss Carew? I suggest you ask President McKinley."

"Perhaps, sir, I should rephrase the question. I understand there is a good deal of cane in Cuba. Would it not be advantageous for the Sugar Trust if the present insurrection led to, let us say, that island's freedom from Spanish rule? Would not a direct relation with the island comfort both the imperialists and the protectionists? Do you not favor a reduction of tariff barriers? Would you not be more amenable to North American colonization of the Caribbean than Spanish?"

"The rapidity of your interrogation, Miss Carew, never ceases to amaze me. I favor, as you undoubtedly know, the Gorman-Price Tariff Bill, which, by restricting the amount of sugar that can be imported into this country, protects American labor. As for colonization, you are very much mistaken in your insinuation. I am now and always have been a good Republican. We are the party of Lincoln, and we are now—whether or not you approve—the party of popular support. Our interest in foreign soil extends only to a defense of the Monroe Doctrine, and completely excludes imperial adventures, whether within or beyond this hemisphere. Does that clarify matters for you?"

"Somewhat. You mean to say that you confine your designs at present to small and relatively defenseless nations near our own shores. You mean to deny that the Dey expedition is yet another imperialistic foray into untapped markets. You mean to deny that greed has any relation to this exotic enterprise, and that your motives in mounting this expedition—"

"Emphatically!"

She had succeeded in annoying him. "Most emphatically do I deny it! Apparently you have lost sight, in your zeal for exposé, of what your editor so decorously labels the 'human element.' Should an expedition be

First it was white, and then it was black, and then: nothing.

A hinted grin over the young man's face. He coughed a single laugh as he allowed himself to fall into a sitting position, head ducked beneath his arms against the wind. The blackness swirled around him, noisy, sharp with pellets, a bristling pandemonium. Was it the cry of vultures above?

Soon, Jed told himself, it would be over.

A painter afforded the vantage of the vultures might have missed seeing the dot that was Jethro Dey amid the stark splendor of the early morning Tibetan landscape. He would have remarked, perhaps, on the precipitousness of the drop from the predator's cliff to the plain below; he might expound on that plain's flatness, on the jagged sweep of the mountains beyond, just now sparkling into dawn; perhaps, if his eyes were especially acute, he might have perceived five figures scattered about a quarter of a mile away from the base of the bluff. But it is unlikely that, through the maddened grating of the wind, he could have made these forms out as the mutilated remains of the Holmohr-Dey Tibetan expedition, the local bandits' latest prize. Nor would he suspect that, of the five that had set out from Kathmandu for Lhasa a month ago four were dead and one, blind and freezing, was now confronting the fact that he would soon join his former companions.

His father, and his mother—if the priests told true. In a little while the fantastic events of the past few months would enter an unwritten history, with none but the vultures to say that on this day sometime in the middle of a Tibetan winter, somewhere in the midst of a great white space, Jethro Dey of New York City, amid corpses of his father and three Nepalese porters, had given his spirit up to the elements.

Was it only last winter they had left New York?

April, yes, had been in Paris, and summer in the Indian Ocean. Then Calcutta, and Kathmandu, and now the great plateau of Tibet. Less than a year, he figured. He reached up again and wiped blood from his head.

Lost, now. All of it. The gold, the medallion, the truth. All of it tribute to the heavy blade of a nameless nomad who would, no doubt, soon barter for *chang* the few pieces of silver he had gained from the slaughter.

One black tooth.

Fat, and sat his horse well. Yak fur at his cuffs. And one black tooth.

The leer flashed into Jed's sightless mind. The weather-rough visage of a man who, in other circumstances, would have been shining the young man's boots. Here, in Tibet, he was chief. Here he bowed to no man; where gold was, he took. Jed saw the smile, the ruffian glee. The blade.

Jed closed his dead eyes against the wind as for the thousandth time he heard the crack of metal against bone, saw a fountain erupt from his father's shoulders, his silver head abob. The son's arms up in protest; a fire, resurgent, into every corner of refuge.

Was that yesterday? Tuesday, he recalled, had been Election Day. So it must have been Wednesday when it happened.

A year ago he had been dancing a gavotte with Jennifer Detroit and looking forward with mild *ennui* to finishing Harvard. Now he was sitting, snowblind, on an icy plateau in the remotest segment of the globe; his father's body, head on its chest, lay under a pile of stones somewhere nearby; in hours Jed would join him.

Deep inside him indignation rose.

It was not the pain so much, not even the terror of dying, that gritted his teeth together. It was the stupidity of it all! Were there a reason, he could be quicker calm, but this . . . it dug at his sense of proportion, his tenacious faith that, however horrendous the getting there, his life must in the end have purpose. French blood, he supposed.

His father's eyes, in that last moment. Not terror, but mere surprise, as a bookkeeper might show at a mistake in sums. As if a violent death were the one unexpected thing, and so, by reason defaulted, an outrage.

He knew how it would be. Years ago he had read it. No: his grandfather had said it. California, the gold fields, and old Charley.

Stiff as a crowbar they brung him in.

Pain, first, as the chill of the skin gives way to a more penetrating chill and the capillaries crystallize. Shirt of fire, Gramp had said: a single agony of fire and ice. Soon after, numbness, loss of motor activity: the first stages of separation from the flesh.

At this point the victim, recognizing that his body has passed a point of no return, launches a last strike for survival. The shirt of fire falls away, but its loss brings no comfort, for the sufferer knows that, his body now beyond him, his mind will soon follow, and then: the end. His conscious mind not yet reconciled to the fate his deeper spirit has already accepted as inevitable, he screams pitiously, beats weakly at the unresponsive flesh, rushes into objects. This erratic motion, however, serves only to aggravate discomfort, for, with agility so severely impaired, he generally only spends energy and hope by inviting assaults to the skeleton.

In any case the process is inexorable. Gradually or abruptly the victim understands this, and then fully, without dubiety, he accepts. Old Charley, Gramp had said, expressed a hesitant joy at this point, confessing a particular attraction for a nearby Ponderosa pine and expiring shortly thereafter, calm as you please.

For most victims, however, there still remain several

37

minutes of consciousness. For perhaps half an hour after the dying man has accepted his lot, he remains quite alert and—it might be said were it not for the lack of visible motion—animated.

It is at this point that the victim's features, apparently without conscious direction, sometimes form that curious arrangement of pressed lips and vacant stare that lead some observers to see in the frozen corpse the figure of a smile. The Yeti grin, said the Nepalese.

Soon the eyes become fixed and the body entirely rigid, and in that frozen aspect the victim passes, at a point no doctor can fix, from life into death.

When he didn't blink no more at my hand, I figgered he was gone.

Soon he would wake. Next to the bed his mother would be setting out cheeses.

She was gone, though, these three years. Acid at the corners of his mouth: for three days straight he had cried. Now, idiotically, he was thankful she would be spared the pain of reading about his death.

Will would read about it in the *Times*. Dear pugnacious Will. His odd, insouciant charm. Jed shielded his eyes against the howling madness of pebbles, and chuckled fondly. What had they meant, all those midnight smokers? Life, fortune, sacred honor: all up on a bet. Who, he wondered, had won the election?

And Jenny.

A sweet claw of memory attacked him. The silk of hair, slope of skin. He fought it back angrily, as false hope.

He would not hear her laughter again, would not be struck, against all of Alec's reservations, at how readily she caught the essence of his confusions. To Will he was linked by mock battles; Jennifer had him by understanding. Alien as the East might have been to her way of life, he had no need to explain his going to her.

38

She alone had not looked incredulous when the journey had been decided.

She would be dancing now, he supposed. Had the season begun in New York? Had McKinley won, or Bryan?

The chill was starting to get to him. He must run. He must keep circulation up.

Shelter. He must find shelter for the night. This endless night around. He could not see, all right, but he could walk, still; he could walk. He could run!

Where?

Anywhere. A rock ledge, a tree, anywhere out of this fury of wind.

Shelter, yes. There would be other nomads by. They would find him. He was not done yet. He could still make it.

The edge of the pit receded, the shirt of fire clung. Every tissue of his body whimpered as the blood went crystal, the hail beat his eyes, the freezing flailed within.

This the horror, then. A scream to waken demons rushed, his mind away, from the throat of the half-frozen boy. There was no taking off the shirt.

In darkness, then, for all. His only sense, hearing; the only sound a roar. Along the fabric of skin, shredding, tears; knives of fire; the horrible shrieks of the damned.

For all eternity.

Among the Norsemen, Alec said, hell was a land of perpetual snow. Cold, he smirked, as hell.

What time was it? Jed clawed at his wrist.

The hands beneath the crystal. What he could not see, he could feel. His right hand swept into the ice, feeling nothing. He raised it before him, cupping.

Squeeze . . . close . . . open . . . again.

A dozen snatches brought nothing, and then—there! He closed his fist greedily about the pebble, worked it slowly, meticulously up between his thumb and forefinger, and struck at his wrist again. The general fire stuck, but now, above the left hand, a new pain. A pain like the pain of his temple, searing deeper and sharp. The pain of an open wound.

Through the heavy mittens Jed could not feel the cut. He hunched closer into himself against the storm and brought the wrist up to his mouth. He opened the crusted lips. In the darkness his tongue found the spot, licked.

The taste of his own blood thrilled him. Warm it was: the blood of a not dead beast. Gingerly he ran the tongue along the flesh, shaking with the excitement of discovery, spun into hope by the saltiness of his own battered skin.

It was not there! His father's gift, too, gone. The timepiece that, strapped to his wrist by a thin band of felt, had so many times elicited amusement from Will and a chuckling approval from Alec—it was gone.

Why should this surprise me? he wondered.

Dark, then.

Calcutta had been hot. Summer, then—or was it always hot in Calcutta? Nepal, perhaps, the fall. Dog-days, Scarfer had said.

Must be November, then. Three months from Kathmandu. Yes: not yet the new year. November.

Election month in New York. Will would be out buttonholing strangers at the Plaza, assuring himself that no Free Silverites had been allowed to slip into that sanctum of Republican virtue. A hollow laugh broke the incessant din of the stones, as Jed realized that even here, on the roof of the world, three miles above the sea, blind and an hour from death, his mind was so knit to the past that he cared, yes cared, who had just been elected president.

The wind was dropping a little. Jed had become so

accustomed to its steady pelting that this small drop in its severity made his torture appear nearly soothing: crouched within the tent of his stiffening limbs, he whispered a nonchalant thanks, whether to the angry god of his fathers, the smiling Buddha of the East, or the capricious hosts of this desolate plateau, he would not have been able to say.

His fingers were starting to go. A light tingling had begun at the tips a moment ago, and already the first joints were beyond him. Jed flexed them quickly, wincing at the pain of even this moderate motion.

It must be night. Even in November, the plateaus were navigable with little more than Alpine gear, and often in the daytime Jed had marveled at the scant garb of porters. At night, however, temperatures here in the Himalayas dropped to 30 and 40 below zero, and against that kind of cold nothing fashioned by the hand of human beings was really serviceable. So, he thought, the tingling taking his hands: it must be night.

Were there stars, then? An odd gust of exultance threw back his head, stretched the stiff lids of his eyes taut, opened his flesh to the wind. Where are you, he surged, Polaris?

But the blackness was total. Unseen sands lashed his wounds, the screaming of a million stones ran fire to his brain. He lowered his head.

His arms hurt now, and his feet. His feet were burning. Hot stones licked his ankles, the knees wobbled. And now all over his body the darts of ice began. The tingling a spiral cloak: it did not carry with it that element of humor that, in the direst situations, the body is generally able to perceive in the sensation of biting cold. It was no teasing now, no bittersweet prick of pain.

A Cape winter: in from snowmen and sleds, his ears a scarlet pinching. *Wait five minutes, dear, it will go away.*

41

But it would not go away. It was a general, insistent fire: reaching for every crevice of his being, eating out the beast, scraping from him all vestiges of doubt, of possibility, investing him only with fear.

In this white blackness. Father, forgive us. He could no longer feel the snow against his flesh. From beneath his knees he scooped up a mittenful and brought it to his face. He felt neither moistness nor cool; had his fist not jarred his head backward, he might have felt nothing at all, for it was only the sudden sharpness of pain from his head wound that alerted him to the fact that flesh and flesh had touched.

The numbness was setting in.

The wind dropped again. The roar had become a dull overhead buzz. Jed opened his useless eyes to the sound and raised his head. He shook an arm: it wobbled as if asleep. He twisted his toes and recognized small, labored movement. The shirt of fire clutched at his throat and sand flayed his eyes and mouth. Coughing, he rubbed the flying irritants into the pupils, blinked stiffly. A new but familiar pain assailed him; briefly he was amused by the superfluousness of sand in his eyes.

Then, sharp and profound, a realization. He could feel! If the duststorm had power still to make his eyes water, numbness had not yet triumphed.

If they watered, they might see!

He would not give it up. Not yet. Some shadowed recollection of incense and dark naves swept through his mind, and his mouth formed the syllables slowly, autonomic:

"Anthony, Mary, Jude."

If I can feel I can see, if I can feel I can stand. He moved his right hand in another circle in the snow. "I can get up," he breathed.

To rise he must pull his legs in under him, rock forward, spring with the knees. The motion a child could perform, for him an act only of grace.

He pulled his knees in close, almost touching his chest. They came in minute and painful increments. It was like cracking ice every inch of the way—and yet, his body was floating.

Jed ground his teeth tight, and they floated, hovered, just short of closed. He could not get them together.

This is a dream; soon, morning.

Somehow, without knowing how his phantom frame had performed the functions, Jed was into a hunch. He could feel no part of his body, yet he knew he had made the first step up. He sat there, immobile in the wilderness, cuddling his knees and staring into blackness, for a space he had no way of measuring.

He had forgotten his home. His friends, those he had loved and those that had loved him, were not even memories. He could have been a stone idol left in the Pleistocene by skinclad wanderers from the North. Amid the corpses in that barrenness, he cast the only shade.

And then the idol moved. Shaking as with all his Jesuitical awe behind, Jed strained his soul toward the single physical task: power he wanted now, no more. Power to unfreeze the plain, power to rise.

The legs were gone. A thousand libations could not unbend them. No amount of prayer or concentration awakened a shiver of sensation. He tried moving his toes but there was no response. Weakly he patted his calves with leaden hands.

Nothing.

Well. If he could not rise, maybe he could fall.

Jed's heart, hammering the stiffening ribcage, shut out the howl of wind as he strained his mind to concentrate on falling. The stone figure shimmered in the dark. It began to shake, to sway.

Vultures might have blinked. Abandon hope, all ye. But then:

Yes!

The idol toppled on to its side. The slight impact jarred the young man enough to give him a new crest of belief. Painfully he stretched his right arm out and pulled himself to his knees. They were locked, or nearly so, and so he could not get up without the aid of his hands. For a moment he let his face rest in the snow. Then, gradually, he pushed his distorted body back so that he was kneeling upright.

He could not stand. His knees locked at right angles, it sapped all his available energy merely to kneel without plunging headfirst into the ice. There, on his knees in the dark, he passed a few regenerative minutes.

What was hell, after all, but a convenience? The worst that can be imagined. Above him pandemonium, black.

He could still make it!

Motion. That was essential. Without mobility he was dead right now. Minutes ago his brain had achieved acceptance, yet now some cellular instinct, some twinge of prerational understanding, the flicker through hopelessness of the ultimate absurdity, faith—stiffened his back and swelled the ice-encrusted flesh into new possibilities.

If he could get moving again, he might make it. Move an inch, rest, and move again. Sustain that and even in this black isolation he had a chance. Fire and sword he had survived this far; might he not triumph now over his own despair?

Move, then! His mind screamed orders to unresponsive limbs. Sand flew about him. He could not tell whether the hood of his parka had fallen off or not; he no longer felt the flying stones. All his dying hope he focused on the blood now gelling in his veins. Get that vital current to move, and he was reprieved.

Only his arms remained. His head wound no longer troubled him, but his arm still ached, and that meant they were not yet stone.

To fall forward. Again a shift of balance, a sway, and the idol dropped down. Palms of ice met the ice of earth. The arms that stopped the fall rattled like bamboo.

Legs locked behind in a misshapen L, Jed began to crawl.

First the right arm, then the left, inched before him to grasp tundra, scrub and snow, to pull the precious earth back and within, to claw him forward into blackness. After each repetition of the pattern he stopped, breathing heavily, before beginning again.

He was going nowhere, perhaps, but he was going. He was not tired. He would not sit still. A caitiff death, that. A man can die on the run!

The wind had died. Jed scarcely noted the change. For half an hour he was a machine, thinking now only of motion. Behind him the weight of invisible, useless limbs; before him one chance in immensity that this creeping progress would bring him, before another night, to shelter, to food, to life. He tried to maintain a straight line.

For god and for gold, Livingston had said. The mocking smile of his grandfather. No, Gramp, not yet. Old Charley must wait for a guest.

But his grandfather had been right. At the root of it was, always, the gold.

If he could make the mountains. Shepherds there. Again the hands reached, pulled, gathered to reach again.

But now he hit something new. Not so smooth, nor

aflame. Jed stopped, kneeling, and bent both hands to the task of blind examination.

It was stone. Jed dropped it, proceeded.

Again, a stone. He spread his palms before him, sweeping.

Three, four. Yes, a pile of them.

His heart rumbled in the cage, his mind fighting to deny what the body already knew. But now it was beyond fabrication. No bell would end this dream.

It was the cairn.

His father's cairn that—was it only yesterday?—his hands had piled up around the man's headless frame. Nearby, Jed knew, were the strewn corpses of the porters.

For a day he had been moving in circles.

He worked his way up the rocks toward the center. His arms swept the air, banging hard into the makeshift cross, and he pulled himself up by its base until he was sitting on top of the pile. He moved the body he could not feel until it was steady on top, his back against the wood.

How many days had it been since, his head on fire, he had clawed these rocks out of the ice, stationed them here against predators? There was no time now, no day and no night. Perhaps it had all happened a long time ago.

The wind had stopped now, entirely. Jed forced his eyes closed, then open again. Light lances of pain skitted through his arms and along his forehead. Involuntarily he clenched a hand, as from out of sleep, against the dark.

It was done. He knew that now. Two days ago, or four, or a generation, he had buried his father here. In all his wandering, he had succeeded only in returning to his grave. With a macabre smugness he allowed himself to lean against the wood and emit a last short spurt of despair. Then he was quiet.

He had the secret now. No hope. An immense wave of relief enveloped him as he realized that his fate had now passed into hands other than his own. He sat there for a few moments, imagining his body emptying itself into the air.

And soon the numbness returned.

This time it was quicker than before. Jed felt his lips press together in a smile he had never formed before as the last vestiges of feeling left his body and his breathing, its purpose resolved, slowed to the near-dead rhythm of the plateau.

It was, at last, the hour.

Fleetingly, he noted the irony of his situation. What millenia of evolutionary design had gone to make up the wretched example of the human species now stiffened into a hieroglyph on this abandoned portion of earth? What fancy or design had seen to it that, five months short of his majority, Jethro Lansing Dey should be spending his last conscious moments staring, continents from home, into an unrelenting dark?

Still he was now, beyond feel. It was a sensation unique in his experience, this state on the other side of control. His mind at last free of doubt, his body no longer his own, he grinned.

An absorbing, lifting lightness took him. He had the impression he was in and out of his body at once. For a moment he saw himself a stone standard, warning errant travellers, and at the same time the planter of that standard, hovering timeless above the wastes and his own empty carcass, chuckling softly as the stone image was reduced by degrees, by weather and scavengers, to dust.

It was beyond him now. No more than nostalgic fondness linked him to Jethro Dey. He was not of the world of men; he was rolling down, calm and stolid; rolling, centuries long, through a million springs to come. He had become the earth. Thought was not. No dreamer and no dream, but only the land, even its pulse.

The stone figure was still. The border had been reached. Now: dawn.

From the pit of his being light began. It swelled through the sinking frame, punched open the eyes. On a horizon immeasurable to men a blue and blinding sea began its ascent. A hundred generations yet unborn, as many ages gone, had contrived to create that sun. The motion of the planet had stopped.

Behind him the sun came up brilliant, casting the shadow of the cross over him and illuminating the three carcasses, already being harrassed by birds, that he had been unable to bury. He was facing West, then. Before him the sun caught first the ragged crest of Dhaulagiri, turning the snow there into a dazzling triangle.

Fire on the mountain. The gold.

And once again he could see.

As he had been the stone, now he was the light. In the deep unfrozen caverns of his being, the image delighted him. He fixed his eye on the mountain and waited to die.

CHAPTER 3

BEAUX ARTS

Soft grey gloves flapped one, two on white linen. Their owner crossed a gabardine knee over its mate and pulled irritably at a trim goatee. One hand pinched linen, the other beat a desultory tatoo on a felt hat resting in the chair to his right. A flash of silver. Manicured fingers rise. A twist of wrist.

"Garçon."

The waiter was busy. He and his colleague were engaged in an animated discussion of last night's bombing. Anarchists, one said; the police, rejoined his friend. All that either of them knew for sure was that sometime around midnight a pipe bomb had been thrown into the Café de la Paix, killing two customers and a waiter and closing the doors of that elegant establishment for the first time in its history. The dead waiter had been a friend, and the crispness of this Paris morning was as a result now being sullied by shared grief and dour speculation. If the boulevards themselves were not immune to attack by these madmen, where then in all the world was safety?

The two were unaware or unimpressed by the impatience of the young man with the goatee. The first of the season's Americans, he could afford to wait. Their inattention increased his agitation, and he tapped a silver spoon lightly, rhythmically against a china saucer to attract their attention. Before him a field of top hats and flowered bonnets swirled gracefully in the late morning light, the easy contentment of their owners' faces betraying no recognition that, two blocks and ten hours away, two of their number had been torn apart by shrapnel.

The young man scanned the scene with mild displeasure, for the waiter was not the only cause of his frustration. It had been an unprofitable morning all around. It was not enough that the mail had been late in arriving at the family lodgings, or that Jennifer, unable to resist an eleventh hour dinner invitation the night before, could not be persuaded to rouse herself this morning until nearly ten. It was not enough that they had already dawdled a month here, when their friends were in the midst of the New York season and Jed was God only knew where. On top of the delay and the boredom that only a Paris out of season could elicit, Will had had to spend the good part of a spring morning trapped in a dusty anteroom in Montmartre, attempting vainly to wriggle information out of that cantankerous woman Blin.

L'Art Nouveau, the sign had read, but the inside was anything but new.

The shop where John Pierre Dey arranged his Parisian transactions was cluttered from floor to ceiling with the cobwebbed flotsam of a lifetime of collecting. One wall was boxes, three deep. Two others, which faced the intersection, held scores of tiny windowpanes, and pressed up against them in a jumble that seemed designed to startle the passerby was a horde of artifacts and statues, lamps and armoires and weavings, that bore all the marks of having been recently wrested from some cavern of the globe where polish was still a thing unknown. Many-armed boddhisattvas rested on carved chests of drawers; chandelier crystal dangled

50

precariously from African lance heads; bits of rhinestone and felt swam underfoot in the dust. In the center of the room, all but blocking passage to the rear, where a gauze curtain separated the shop from the proprietess's quarters, stood an enormous display case: under glass that could not, Will reckoned, have been cleaned since the Commune, was a trove of colored lights. Beryl and amethyst and crystal and gold: here in this dirty Montmartre closet, a continent removed from the hands that had fashioned them, they sat awaiting shipment to Fifth Avenue, Park Lane, L'Etoile.

From out of this mélange of Orientalia and dirt stepped a small stocky woman clutching a ragged shawl and squinting through the poor light. Behind the display case she stopped, resting meaty hands on the glass. Her neck bent slightly to the right and a pair of puffy eyes blinked twice, deliberate, as if in coded welcome.

"So," she said hoarsely, "you are the friend of Dey."

"Jethro Dey is my friend, Madame." Automatically the felt hat tipped into one hand, while the other withdrew a slim calling card from a vest pocket and placed it between the woman's hands on the glass.

Only a spurt of air betrayed her amusement as, with exaggerated delicacy, she picked the card up by its edges and brought it close to her face. A quick pout of approval, and the card flipped cleanly out of her hands to rest, face up, on the glass in front of its owner.

"*Alors,* Monsieur William Parkinson Detroit the Two, what can I do for you?"

Will retrieved the card and returned it to its pocket. "I am told, Madame Blin, that you may have information regarding the recent disappearance of my friend and his father from Paris to Tibet. I understand there is a man by the name of Haji—"

"Hajib. *Oui*. Mustafa. The trader of the white gold, yes?"

"Hajib. Yes, yes. I understand you may know where I can contact this man."

The woman's head shot back and a mouth lacking a bicuspid opened in mirth. "Find Hajib? Contact Hajib, eh? Will you contact the wind? Do you know where are the snows of last December? Why," she was abruptly grave, "do you wish to find the Arab?"

The young man's hands parted in an expression he supposed to be one of Gallic complicity. Why was this woman being difficult? "Because, Madame," he began slowly, "he is my only connection to my friend and his father, outside of you yourself, anywhere between here and the East. I am anxious to find my friends, but Asia is a large place, and I would be more than grateful for a clue as to where to begin looking."

"Begin looking. Ah." Mme. Blin's arms sought the rafters. "In all of Asia, then, only the Arab may know this? Ah, Americans . . ."

She was silent for a moment. Digesting, it looked to Will. He waited. In a minute the large eyes narrowed at him.

"I have been in Brittany until yesterday," she said.

"I know that, Madame. I have been in Paris for three weeks awaiting your return, because I had been led to believe that you could furnish me the information I needed. Am I correct in understanding that you are the friend and business associate of John Pierre Dey of New York City, and that you are familiar with the schedule of his travels?"

"Do not insult me with courtesy, my friend. You come in here and demand an Arab. I am thinking. Wait."

Will ran a grey glove along the wooden molding of the case, then let the hand drop as inconspicuously as possible to his side, fighting down the urge to wipe the dust off on the underside of the case. Was it really conceivable that John Pierre could have entrusted his Paris dealings to this sweaty Bretagnaise? Perhaps he had the wrong shop.

"Fill in the spaces, my friend. I have been away. Disappeared, you say, lost. No Dey I know has ever been lost. Explain."

Patiently, Will gave the woman the outline of his plight. Gradually she became sympathetic, concerned. She seemed genuinely surprised to learn that, after passing through Paris some six months ago, neither father nor son had sent back to America more than the most perfunctory communication. Will warmed to her slightly as he realized that her initial harshness had been the result not of nastiness but of ignorance. As he concluded the sketch with the pained admission that, since last summer, only Jed's curt mailgram had given any indication of the whereabouts of the two travelers, Mme. Blin's face twitched faintly. Staring eyes dropped.

"Tibet? A cold country."

"So I understand. Well, that is where they were going, the last anyone heard. Can you help me?"

"Tibet." The woman mused, glum. "To go all the way to Tibet because a man with the Byzantine fancy must have the gold—this is very strange. Look here."

She produced a small key from her bosom. Beneath the glass a click. Rusty hinges. The lights danced.

From a corner of the horde she extracted a small medallion, flipped it to Will. He caught it in cupped hands, rubbed the surface, nodded.

"Pretty, yes."

"Yes," she replied. "Pretty. Except to a dozen eyes between here and Istanbul, this is no different from the piece that has brought our friends so far from home.

This is gold, my friend. But it is not *the* gold. You understand?"

Will returned the piece. "I am afraid I have little eye for jewelry. Gold is pretty much gold, to me."

"No one," her voice dropping conspiratorially, "would take himself to Tibet for this. But the gold of Hajib. That is a very special gold. There is much strangeness in that gold."

The mention of the Arab's name heartened the young man, for it suggested that in spite of her discursiveness the woman was not entirely unaware of the issue at hand. What of Hajib, then? Did she know where he might locate the Arab?

"Arabs," she said quietly, "are to be found everywhere. In Paris there are Arabs. In Algeria, in Istanbul. If you are looking for Hajib you might go to Istanbul; often he is in Istanbul in the summer. But I think this is not wise. Hajib is a great liar. He would point you wrong for the amusement of it. Did you not say Calcutta? Tibet? Why have you need of Hajib? Take a packet to Calcutta, a road to Tibet."

"Tibet is a large country. Where do I look?"

The woman sighed. "I will tell you about Tibet. Once, perhaps twice in a decade, a white person enters Tibet and is permitted to remain. If your friend and his father have gone there, they will surely have been noticed. You do not need the Arab. Go to Kathmandu. Ask in the streets, in the cafés. They will have passed through Nepal, and the people will remember. Would you like some coffee?"

The waiter's face was impassive. Will rose from reverie long enough to tap his empty demitasse with the side of a silver spoon and murmur "S'il vous plaît." Instantly the china was gone, the waiter in retreat to the kitchen. The knifecrease knees recrossed themselves, the gloves resumed the tattoo.

Where in the devil was she? Trust a woman to botch it, he twitted, the chide not so much against his sister as against himself for allowing her to sleep in. Eleven, was it? Half past, more likely. Irritably he yanked the chain, popping the silver timepiece out, and flicked the lid that had been engraved for him on his twenty-first birthday by old man Tiffany himself. The long arm had dropped just past the three. Will sniffed, drubbed it shut with his thumb.

Let her sleep, then. She needed it, he supposed. He was frankly glad to see his sister escaping the remorse and uncertainty that had so pressed her down since Jed disappeared. He was pleased that Jenny's spirits seemed to have been boosted by Paris in bloom. His sister was young, and pretty, and—after all—a woman. It would not do for her to pine morbidly after a man who, everyone admitted, might have very little chance of ever returning to her. Yes, it was right she should be distracted now. He smiled involuntarily, as his second coffee arrived, at the recollection of last night's merriment. The waiter, thinking the smile was meant for him, withdrew with some confusion.

It had been a fine ball. Nothing, of course, like the Astors', but a party of much charm and with, he supposed, as much distinction as could be expected from Europe's peculiarly provincial *beau monde*. There had been no scattered clacques of millionaires such as graced every gathering of the New York 400; no bedizened matrons, oozing politesse and rich fragrance; no nightlong feasts complete with six aspics, too much cognac, flutes. Paris took its pleasure more moderately, and Will had to confess he liked the more relaxed atmosphere.

And Jenny had had a fine time! Dancing from dusk till near dawn with that baron fellow, what was his name? Began with an A. Good catch, as their mother would say—for a Frenchman.

Yes, it pleased him to see his sister happy again. A year was long enough to grieve for the departed. His father's counsel he had taken to heart: if it was nothing, then nothing would come of it; if something, then it could withstand a twelve-month hiatus. As single-minded as Jenny had remained right through the ocean voyage, it gave him a considerable lift to see his advice taken now, and the girl busying herself with the diversions that were proper to her station and the season. The eccentricities of the Paris set aside, it was grand to see her once again a center of urbane admiration.

He wondered, though, if he had not done his job too well. There was a balance to be maintained, and Will was not certain that Jenny's late emergence from her self-imposed hibernation had not been accomplished at the price of a certain reserve. There were many, he was aware, who might consider her midnight escapade with the young aristocrat a subject for speculation if not censure, and he was eager to give no one grounds to suspect either her virtue or his diligence. Dancing till dawn—was that not stretching the proprieties a little far?

Jed, after all, was still lost, and no one they had yet encountered could say with conviction that he and John Pierre were not both dead. Will was hardly ready to don sackcloth himself; but he felt the requirements of decorum a bit more strongly than other young men of his class. He would speak to her about it.

Her intentions aside, it was damned annoying to be kept waiting here, a sullen waiter over his shoulder, and nothing to read.

And where the devil was Jed?

Glumly he reminded himself it had been well over a year since he had last seen his friend, more than six months since anyone in New York had received anything but discouraging notes from the two travellers. His Roman faith sent murmurings to the skies. His scientific mind, though, stopped. Was it reasonable to suppose that, after six months of silence and only the thin suspicions of a Madame Blin to go on, he would have any success in tracking down, somewhere in the wastes of Asia, two wayward Americans?

If they were still alive.

But it was not reason that had sent Will on this journey, no more than reason had sent Jed and John Pierre on theirs. It was, rather, an odd complicity of motives that had hoisted the young man out of New York just at the height of the season and deposited him, impatient and chafing with frustration, at this linen-decked, fin de siècle table. Will's cavernless mind was, to be sure, not privy to the complicity. Had you asked him what he was doing in Paris, the reply would be direct and without dubiety: "I am," he would say, "on my way to Tibet. A friend of mine is there. I must bring him home."

Good enough, one might concede, for a simple man. Yet Will was not quite simple. His motives, if unmurky, were complex; one would misread him to suppose the whole of his impulse was a twining of affection and rectitude. He might have jumped into dragons' lairs for the sake of a father or a friend; but he'd do it for more than the necessity.

He was straight enough, all right; it might indeed be said of him that duty had become an instinct. This meant he was above all a man to be relied on. And yet there was more to it.

For Will had been reared on strong milk. The son of the corporate aide had ingested, in those straining years of hope and industrial design, more than his share of the desperate, glorious dreams of youth. Afternoons of

57

charges and austere encampments with Jed in Central Park had made a strong impression on him. By the time he was fourteen he had decided on a military career. Even without the bangles and the braid, the soldier was, to his bright adolescent mind, the embodiment of all noble virtue, all duty and grandeur and esteem. The tale of Gordon at Khartoum he had devoured avidly; Kipling was his bedside favorite, and many a night he had wept into his pillow over the sad and glorious end of Custer at the hands of the Sioux.

He welcomed this journey, therefore, as a means of escape and adventure as well as a responsibility. William Senior had made it plain that, upon his graduation, the patronage of the Sugar Trust would extend to him; thus he was assured of a profitable and honored position immediately upon leaving New Haven. Perhaps this journey, then, was to be the last fling he would have for some time. He welcomed it appropriately, with a gusto that someone less well provided for might not so readily feel.

It was no lark, to be sure. There were Stanley and Burton before him. He felt the burden of a short but stirring tradition. The fact that Jed was in danger, and might bring that danger yet down on him, only increased his appetite for the job.

Well, then. A year gone. The ocean in winter, Paris in the spring, the summer yet to be revealed. He fidgeted again, draining the coffee cup, and looked out over the street.

Jenny was nowhere in sight. Will allowed his eyes to range over the expanse of color and motion that gave its shimmering quality to the life of the boulevard. Top hats bobbed regular as pistons; parasols twirled, flecking sunspots; a thousand flowered bonnets swayed five feet from earth, a stupendous elevated garden; here and there, buggies delivered sightseers, horses snorted, spirited in the brisk April air.

It was a peaceful town, he mused. Without the excitement of his own, and without the anxieties too. Were it not for the urgency of his task, he might stick it here awhile. Jed, he remembered, had always spoken well of Paris. What was it he called it? A city of exquisite ennui.

He found her, finally, coming through the throng a queen among peasants. She had on one of the loose white shirtwaists being worn this season in New York. There they had already gained both prominence and a name as a result of the esteem in which they were held by the redoubtable Mrs. Henry Dana Gibson. Here, where the Gibson look had not yet had a chance to challenge the hegemony of grey twill, high collars, and low bustles, Jennifer's costume would have attracted attention even if she were merely standing on a corner. Weaving through the crowd, however, with the whiteness shifting undulant against her long, lean thighs; with the simple tan skimmer accentuating at once her auburn crown, her carriage, her height—here she was a figure to be reckoned with. Will grinned inwardly as twisting necks told him that he was not alone in holding his sister a paragon of the new American womankind.

Her face was raised to the sun, and a smile of infinite innocence caressed her features. She walked indolently, easily, as if she were entirely unaware that she had already kept her brother waiting the better part of an hour. She is blithe, he thought, and so oblivious. She does not know they are looking at her. She barely knows where I am.

At first this lackadaisical gait annoyed him; then, as so often in the past, he became a happy victim to the sparkle that Jenny, when she was happy, had the ability of showering on an unwitting world. Yes, she had him all right. Bemused, chastened, delighted, he folded the gloves, lay them on the table, eased the grillwork chair next to him away from the table.

She was a couple of cafés down. Her parasol, draped over her arm, had caught in the rung of a chair. Instantly four masculine hands were at her service; the offending metal was detached; a flurry of smiles all around; and the princess again on her way.

"Jennifer!"

Brightly, she turned.

"Willie!"

The diminutive irked him briefly; he let it pass. "Won't you sit down, mademoiselle?"

Mock gallantry pulled out the chair, flourished over the seat an imaginary cloth. Will took a special glee in the small display, aware that every male eye on the boulevard was upon him. Demurely, a nod: she sat.

"I don't suppose," he said, "you'd care to explain?"

Jenny lay the parasol, white like her dress, across the arms of the table's third chair and brushed an auburn strand out of her eyes. "Explain?" Genuinely surprised, and then: "Oh, that? This? Willie, I am truly sorry. Fully, Willie, I am. Last night was—well, you know, so *long*—and it wasn't, I think, till past ten that Mireille got me up. It can't be past twelve now, can it? All things considered," she concluded, bright brown eyes quizzing his watch, "I think I've done a fair job."

The smile was infectious and, so long had it been since he'd seen it, irresistible. "Damn it, Jenny," he said lamely, dutifully, "I've been in this café for an hour. Could of had three breakfasts by now. Do you think—"

"Vin blanc," she said, calm. Behind Will the waiter bowed, then, his eyebrows raised in question, gestured toward him.

"Deux," Jenny supplied. He was gone.

"Will . . ." No rings yet on her hand. Firmly it

rested on his. "Do you think," her thin brows knit, "I should not have gone with Aristide?"

A clasp, quickly, fraternal.

"Who?"

"Aristide. The baron, you remember. Or were you," she chided, "too far gone?"

"I was not too far gone!" The vehemence of his reply surprised him. "The baron, yes, I remember him. A good enough sort, I suppose. I only wonder whether you should be . . ."

Those guileless, expectant eyes. He would have to, he saw, spell it out.

"Well, damn it, should be . . . should you be out all night with this fellow, after all? We don't know him, really. Where he comes from, who his people are . . ."

"His people? Oh, Will. Dear Will."

"Now what is that supposed to mean?"

Smoothing the front of her dress. The unperturbed gaze of the schoolmarm, debating the fractious child. "I don't care about his people, Willie. I only care about his . . . about his . . ."

"Yes?" The suspension annoyed him.

"His feet."

Her brother's splutter of picque was muffled by the arrival of the waiter. "Deux vins blancs, m'sieur-dame."

Will waited until the man was out of earshot. Then he turned, aggravated, to his sister. "What do you mean, his feet?"

Sighs. Of recognition, of calm, of unflustered despair. Of knowing at last that it would never be any other way with her brother. Then: "Dancing, Will. Dancing! He is without a doubt the finest dancer I have ever met. And he knows the new ones, too! All those mazurkas and reels! Thank God they are obsolete here. Here it's all moonlight and dreams, the dances of beautiful death, the melodies of gold and musk and paradise—am I losing you, Willie, dear?"

"Yes," he admitted. "What I am getting at, dear sister, is that we—you and I—are engaged at the moment on a journey to bring our friend back from wherever the devil he may be in Asia. What do you think," he ended solemnly, "Jed would think of all this?"

He thought he had caught her off guard and introduced the proper note of sobriety into this intoxicating Parisian morning. But then the dark eyes lowered.

"I think it's damned unfair of you, Will, to do that to me."

"Unfair?" he said, hurt himself.

"It's not," she said, sipping the wine, "as if I've neglected him."

"No, no, not that," he mused, sipping his own. "I didn't mean that, Jen. It's just that I think people—"

"Might talk," she finished, acridly.

"Perhaps," he gave in. He did not begrudge her her flights of fancy with this unknown nobleman. The Lord knew she had been diligent enough in her grief. Maybe he was overdoing it. Their father would be overjoyed she had taken an interest in another man. While he knew he could not, for the sake of his friendship with Jed, endorse that, he did not want to be in the position of denying it to her. Let him take the burden, then, and leave her to Paris and spring.

"I'm sorry," he said abruptly. "I do know how you care for him."

"Yes," the girl replied. "Yes, I care for him. How did you make out at Madame Blin's?"

Swiftly he related the tale of his unsuccess, feeding her just enough good tidings that she would not entirely lose hope. When he was finished she nodded.

"So we're off to Kathmandu?"

"I'm going alone," he said.

"You're afraid I will be a burden."

"No. The country is dangerous. There is no certainty, no communication, no police. It's no place for a white woman, that's all."

She smirked and for a moment Will was caught in memory. Her face bore an expression he had seen many times before: a cast of amused resignation that she used to adopt whenever he and Jed discussed war in her presence. It never failed to make him uneasy.

"Would you really want to go?"

The smirk passed. "I suppose not. But I'd prefer to make the decision myself."

"Well," he stammered, "I'm sorry if I've—"

"Don't be sorry, Will. It doesn't become you. I'm quite aware at this point of where I'd be a help and where I'd not. You see," she winked, "I've not entirely forgotten who I am. Who we are. Do me one favor, though."

"Of course."

"Don't get yourself killed."

"Killed?" The laugh of the grenadier. "Don't be silly, Jen. If they're to be found, I'll find them. If not . . ."

It was no Gallic shrug, but it passed.

"Willie." She leaned close, quiet. "Why are you doing it?"

"Why?" The question had not occurred to him in such simplicity.

"For me? For yourself? Or for Jed?"

"You know, I really can't say. Something I have to do, I guess, but I don't know why."

He frowned, was suddenly sharp. "Why the devil did he have to go to Tibet in the first place? Holmohr wouldn't know Indian gold from Parisian if you packaged it right. Sometimes I get so mad at him . . ."

"Yes," she agreed. "But it could not have been any other way. He's like you in that."

"I don't understand."

"You have to go find him. He had to go in the first place. Maybe it was written," she quipped.

"Oh, not that damned fatalism stuff now, Jenny! It doesn't explain a thing. There's no reason he should have gone. He had everything in New York."

"Perhaps he didn't want everything."

"Well, what on earth *did* he want?"

She leaned back in the chair and swirled the wine. A drop jumped, stained the cloth, and she smiled. Her look of resignation, of a humor beyond all their fates, returned.

"Nothing, perhaps. Nothing at all."

CHAPTER 4

DREAMDUST

It was not finished.

Spine flat against the wood cross, eyes unable to move from the dazzling triangle, Jed dove through amazement and fear to the hollows of the past, dredged out of the unfrozen recesses of mind a curt and blasphemous challenge.

Non consummatum.

Royal purple, beeswax, gold. The bite of frankincense in his brain.

It was a Sunday afternoon. Mass had gone out at noon. He had walked leisurely west from the Avenue to the Park, pausing an hour in the Metropolitan to wonder at the prominence the trustees had accorded his father's latest gift, and then proceeded through the February mud to his own secluded knoll, and the tree.

The park had not yet greened, but the big elm sported, here and there along its massive limbs, the hard tiny bumps hinting budding. In a month the lacery of bark and branch would flourish a translucent green; a fortnight more and the canopy would be complete—thick emerald leaves, drooping seedpods, wind in her hair. Jed ran his hand down the trunk smiling as chips of bark dusted his wrist and the cuff of his camel coat. Greedily he breathed the subtle freshness; even and deep, once, twice, three times, until his nostrils had forgotten the pungency that had clung to him from church. Then he stripped open the buttons, flung the expensive garment at the foot of the tree, and sat.

Gnarls bit his spine, and he shifted until he found comfort. Then he placed his wrists upon his knees and closed his eyes.

Three thaws he had sat out here. The tree had become a benchmark: an abiding presence against which, no matter how dreary the day, the boy had been able to measure the oddly impersonal beauty of seasonal change. This would last. He trusted the tree in a way he could trust no person. Not Will, not Alec, not Jenny, was able to command from him the uncomplicated allegiance he felt to . . . to what?

Not God, certainly. Or better: not the Christ. Not his father's god, then. Nobodaddy, perhaps, wreathed with rules and burnings.

But Jesus is your best friend.

Why that? Jesus a statue, a painted window. He lived on Park Avenue north of the station, in an exquisitely decorated house with other statues. Jed knew their names: Thérèse and Francis, and John. Cousins of stone, it was not them he knew.

It was not the risen son the elm brought him to, but something more amorphous: that which could not be drawn. Something along the blood, and not in the head.

The fires of hell, my son.

Was it fear, then? Only that? Jed breathed again, deep and sound, and opened his eyes. A black streak before him settled on a rock. "Should of been a blackbird," he hummed, "hanging in a tree."

Seventeen, this spring. A something between wincing and a smirk drew tight the young man's mouth, and he shifted again so that the ragged bark nestled into the other half of his back. *When,* he wondered to the bird, *did I begin to lose it?*

It was not fear, exactly, that embraced him. More a kind of vague intellectual terror, as if the loss of faith were a matter rather for the psychologist than the priest. And all conviction gone: the simple chilling words of Donne fluttered by. "Not the terror of the pit could be more perfectly awful to this supremely rational Christian than the discovery, gleaned out of hours of rigorous inspection, that the story of his god was a lie."

He supposed he should be afraid. Deny your lord, and die. Was that it, then? The father would say it so, and Jed had inherited enough of the older man's Gallic sentiment for the One True Church to comprehend the emotions that were, at this juncture of failing belief, appropriate if not heartfelt. The nostalgic tug was there, all right, and lord knew he wanted to believe, firm enough. But an adolescence full of the Bhagavadgita and Nietzsche, a term of young manhood spent (wasted, Will would say) at freethinking Harvard, and the dim but fervent memory of his proudly agnostic grandfather had conspired to wean out of Jed all but the merest trace elements of remorse for his disavowal of the Faith.

Like getting something caught between your toes that no amount of shaking can dislodge—that was the way he saw it now. A constant aggravation, no more. He could walk with it, well enough, and it could hardly, at this stage, be considered painful; yet it annoyed him, no denying it, annoyed him just enough to make each step a little bit of a chore.

He wondered if time would ameliorate or worsen the condition. Would he learn to live with the burr, and become in time only faintly amused by the tickle it sent up toward his spine? Or would the annoyance turn with the years to torture and, like the bastinado, drive him mad through the soles?

Time, they would say, would tell.

What you don't feel along your spine, Gramp had

said, no amount of drill will ever convince you of . . . and it was not—had not been for a long time—along his spine. The twitch worked into a rueful grin and the young man sniffed again the resurgence of earth that now, late youth going fast, had replaced Romanism as his one abiding conviction. He was comfortable under this tree: emptiness almost, and so the comfort of the lost.

It was easy, however, to be fooled by the season.

Out of the serpent's mouth, a tail. Before him not a blackbird, but Dhaulagiri. A slippage in the circle, a twitch of fate: this was Tibet, and Jethro Dey was afraid. In that shimmering state between awake and dream, he stirred. Not the blackbird, not the tree. The form was massive, his situation clear.

Dhaulagiri, the holy mountain, swelling in sunlight. He below, stiffening to die.

He could not feel his body at all, but was vaguely conscious of the flurry of dust still battering the Tibetan wastes around him. He was obscured from the vulture's view by now, so constant had the whirling winds become.

Before him the peak of the prophet. He would not reach it now, and it amused him briefly: he was grateful that the hidden gods of this plateau had seen fit, at the hour of his death, to give him dawn. Dawn on the October hills. The country was far away.

India! Thoreau had said . . .

He had for a moment the sensation of being able to push the crazed particles, the awful scrim of the world, away from him merely by willing it so. A curious wave of power swept him as he realized the extent of his isolation, his hopelessness, his—despair, was it? No, not that. Something cruder than a schoolman's notion, something cool and exhilarating along the blood.

A good sneeze, said the Indians, cleared the brain.

The horizon shifted, dropped. Sliding on the axes of the earth, the massive forms moved back. A million centuries dropped.

Pleistocene the cold.

He was the last of the race. The final painter, composing this clean desolation. He was pleased, briefly, by the burden.

Across the river a new form moved. Black, small, coming fast. Jed could not make it out until, its eyes reflected in the moon silver of the river, it flashed to him in lights:

It was a bear.

He realized he had perhaps a minute to live. The black form bounded comical, monstrous, across the plain and dug into the stones at the foot of the rise where Jed sat. For a minute it halted, as if confused, and raised a quizzical snout toward him. Come, then, Jed whispered. Make it quick. All his muscles were rigid with the effort not to scream. Terror ate its way up his body as the beast approached, still hesitantly curious about the still form against the cross. It nosed among the rocks, reached out a huge paw, grazed Jed's knee. The terror had caught at the throat, he felt himself floating away, a black light surging, whirling. The bear raised up.

The beast stood eight feet high. Three-inch claws protruded from matted fur. A mouthful of daggers, eyes of flint, the breathing ragged, foul and hot. The jaws would surround the young man's skull as easily as a squirrel cracked a nut. Six hundred pounds of prehistoric hunger lumbered toward him.

Blood of the martyrs—

Legs too small for the monster's weight. A dancer's toes. Calves bent, flexed, and the bear's enormous paws swam through the frozen air toward his eyes.

He met the beast's eyes without reasons, locked his

gaze there, wanting to meet his death awake and, just beyond the final terror, smiling.

But it froze. The claws hovering, the wood against his spine.

It was not Jed who blinked. Something blinked inside him. He was beyond control. When his eyes opened he was staring at miracle: the bear was frozen too. The claws still, the teeth still, spittle crackling, aglisten in the emptiness. And the glacial, hungry eyes—gone!

Amazed, Jed watched the giant predator disintegrate. First fell the fur: in great matted clumps it splotched the snow, turned into a hundred scurrying rodents, fled. The muscles next, and the organs. One by one the sinews, heart, the stomach that could have held him whole, a grey fuzz of brain, the vining net of blood, ran off into the snow, until only the bones remained.

Eight feet above the tundra, the huge sockets, the browning, stiffened fangs. Within the ribcage, nothing. The dancer's toes a frieze of tiny bones. In a second the weight of the massive structure would topple it forward onto him.

To be crushed by a framework of bone . . .

No beast had heard the laugh. Jed alone heard it. In the deeps of his stomach it rolled as, for a moment, he understood. Windchimes, crystal rattle, the sound of absurd delight . . . and the skeleton too was gone.

Before him in the snow only a pile of dust, already being scattered across the river by the wind, told Jed where the monster had been.

To fight the monsters of the flesh you need bullets and knives. To fight the monsters of your mind you need only—your mind. Alec's observation caught him, and again the deep hunger rolled, squealed, pitched him into delight.

And now, again, the mountain.

I am become the earth, he thought. The sunlight and I are the same.

The sun was full on Dhaulagiri. The peak of the mountain, burnt gold. A color of gold Jed had seen but once before. Hajib's gold. The thought wrinkled his eyes, he rubbed at them to awaken, but in vain. It was gold had brought them to this desolation, and gold as he was leaving it. Well, he had got his gold.

The sun in this dawn, the mountain crystal, the jewel of the world: he would die, content.

Shuddering in sleep.

The mana of this world.

He could see only the mountain. Its top aglow, anvil to heaven. The peak afire first, red, then that incomparable gold. Now white, white as bone.

And without a sound, the explosion. Somewhere off, gongs. The mountaintop in air, a thousand fragments hailing. In great gelid rivers of brimstone Dhaulagiri flew, and the fires swept, drooled down the mountain toward him.

The hail of stone was soundless, and painless the deluge. Brief humor tickled him as he realized that fire had no more power over him than ice. It felt free to be dead: a clean, honest ending.

Near the edge of the pit . . .

In the plain before, activity. The eruption had stopped. Dutch peasants in the square, a carnival.

No. Tibet. Kin of lava, kin of stone: the plain was alive with demons.

Monkey gods, feathered and crowned, ogresses and yetis. Screams of pained delight issued from the throng, lewd laughter rose to urge him down. A creature with pointed ears and a single monstrous eye approached him. "Choose!" it cried. Squatting, its right arm splayed toward him a kindly, flickering snake. Its left arm above, a rattler.

That subtle poison to drive the dreamer mad.

In the middle of the circle below, four figures stood bartering. "Leave the boy and take the gold." His father's voice was even, neither pleading nor insistent, To his right Jed stood, a pawn now, a prize. The bandit with one black tooth slid the scimitar from the scabbard.

His father's head, a cup.

Scarfer stood by as the blade sought Jed's neck next. The sailor in the skies wept ice tears, the actor jerked his head away. Fire along the spine, white irons in the brain. Do I sleep or wake?

Against the cross, still. They carried the two heads up to him, his father's and his own. Slowly across the ice-swept earth they trudged across the river, across the plain, bearing to him the fruits of their killing.

No! He must not take it. He must get away! And as sure as Jed was of the terror in his mind, he knew too there was no way out. Straining terrified at last, he exerted the last will left to him in an effort to control his body.

He was dead weight, no more.

In seconds the demons would be up the hill, as his feet. He would be eaten by worms.

He had to scream, but no sound comes. Perhaps, he smiled, I am already dead. And imagined his entire body shaking like grass in a wind, running to a release unlike any he had known.

A love for you no Power can deny.

Now and at the hour of our death . . . I am the resurrection.

False, all! All caitiff hope!

He was shaking, screaming, crying, a leaf torn and done. All the terrors of a Jesuit boyhood, flocking home. Blood of the martyrs, protect me! His body at the edge, would explode.

And then, quite abruptly, it was over. Straining against the bonds which knit him to the cross, he felt as if they had been suddenly, inexplicably, cut. His body lurched forward, and every bilious fluid wound out of him like sunshine out of burning wood. For a second it was Spring, and he understood.

The demons laid a single head before him. The blackbird lighted on the rock. It was, he saw, the head of them both. Two mad Americans seeking gold, he and his father somewhere horribly off the track in Tibet.

The blacktoothed bandit picked the head up, passed over it with his hand. It turned into a skull. Again the bandit's hand passed over it, and it was a cup. A third time and the cup was full.

A black, steaming liquid, the scent of herbs. Jed knew now there was no way out of it, and he reached for the grim vessel, draining it in one draft.

Instantly he was afire. The cup in his hands was a head again, the hair smoking, the skin rapidly curling, black.

"Like your finger in the flame, forever."

But it was not that. Not yet. An instant, the shirt of flame. Another, and the head alone was aflame. He was holding it, burning, yet there was no pain.

Was he not yet dead?

The flaming vessel became an orb, and brilliant again as the mountain. Snowgold, they had said. Jed could not take his eyes from it.

But then it was gone, and in its place a stone. Deep-green, catseye. He looked down, and the green eye grinned. An explosion of light in his hand, dust and starshine in the air.

Then: white, winter light, and the mountain restored. The demons vanished, and Dhaulagiri sparkled in the Tibetan dawn. The sun had caught a good third of it by now, and the shining presence commanded the scene royally as befit its legends.

Jed had the fleet sensation of possibility: he knew that, somehow, he was able to move. But—why he could not say—he had no desire to do so.

The wind had stopped, the ground was green. For the first time since the attack, Jed noticed the river. Before him in the plain, it sparkled smooth and crystalline, catching the mountain's fire and flashing it on up to him, a stream of molten light. Later he would bathe. Now he breathed deep, jasmine and musk and early thaw, and set his sight on the peak.

The golden eye of the sun! That incomparable gold! Thrumming in another life: the only thing in the world was this dawn.

The mountain looked back now. From the center of the triangle an eye: green as his own, and still. Behind the eye:

A man.

He was an old man, unrobed. His skin hung on him like the draping of a statue, moved like marble folds as he walked easily, unhurriedly, across the water. As he approached, Jed saw that his face had the same tent-like aspect, as if behind a thin veil of flesh only a skeleton abided. A monstrous kind of beauty. Jed was calm, unafraid.

The man stood before him. In the center of his forehead, an eye, Green, silent fire. Jed's single eye met it, held. The air was sweeping away, they were two alone, one alone, on dead ground.

The gongs had stopped. The syncopated singing of children filled space. The creature's face began to change, the skin going taut and smooth. It shrunk back to the frame, and he was young. Tight of muscle, clear sparkling eyes, full breath. He was neither man nor

74

woman, then, and both. The dreamer laughed in revery that here there was no shame.

He was a woman, shadowed. A picture to wake from, the Venus astride a huge bat. Jed felt neither desire nor distaste, only a wan gentle pressure of smiles.

He accepted it all. Smiling cooly, he watched the run of forms before him, the great and final dancing of the world: the old man had become the child, and changed he remade the earth, the heavens, everything. Jed looked with rapt and chilling glee:

He was a hooded executioner, framed by faggots and knives. The direct awful Jesuitical image: the bound victim, the sacrificial knife raised, the flames at his feet. Savonarola, then: done.

Jed in purgatory, a dweller there: this Sisyphian stillness his own, the game he has been entrusted to play by the last angry gods he had known.

He was a red man, the fangs of slavery out. Savage miscomprehension, his head on a tomahawk's end. Stories of brained children, and the glitter, the horrible sensual glitter, of the pit. Non-men, these, he knew. Or so he had been taught. Now he began to see it: beyond the sentiment of liberalism, why Indians! had been Thoreau's last word. He would go, and willing, past Sin.

Green, then: the great god Pan returned. Willow staff and his ancient grey head a tangle of thorns, lotus weed, springs. The tingling seductive goat-god. Yes, he would go with that. Scapegoats they set out here: a gift to propitiate the mountains, have them cease their rattling. All right. Curious crackle of delight, the last ribbon of Catholic tangle trailing. It was funny, finally to have become the Christ. Animals, finally, he accepted.

The old man then, again. The grey grand eyes, the streaking yellow hair: Jed exhaled, a pass of easy air going just through him. It would be all right to die with this man.

Then: the man was twenty feet high. No fear, now, as the stranger swelled to phantasm: a Titan now, and the breathing of fire within. Full and risen as the sun he seemed, his clear eyes beckoning without restraint.

Jed would say: Yes.

But again the form changed.

The slip at the gates of the city, Bunyan's most terrible truth. For the instant Jed wavered, the form pitched again. This time a demon, sure. Blue skin, a flurry of arms and heads. Holding him to a dancing body. In a circle they moved, and five heads laughed. The two-backed, wondrous beast.

Around the creature's waist, a garland of skulls; in his hand, suddenly, a cup. The skull of his father, drink! But the creature smiled; and anger was only a jest; and he would take the cup, and drink, and die well.

Two snakes sought each other's mouths.

And it changed.

He was an old man again. Not the grotesque figure of a moment before, but a calm-eyed Indian of possibly three-score and ten, dressed in a tan robe and sandals. His grey, shoulder-length hair was parted vaguely in the middle, and a moderately unkempt mustache and beard hung toward his chest in a small inverted triangle. His eyes were grey as well, and softly inquisitive.

Was it snow or sunlight? Jed had lost the season and the place.

From around his neck the old man unslung a cloth pouch. His hands moved quickly and smooth. Unclasping a gold pin, he removed a bundle of dried herbs from the pouch, wrapped them in a square of white cloth which he then rubbed on the frozen ground and, with a length of string, secured to the center of Jed's forehead.

Their eyes met. Jed was not afraid. He wanted to

speak, could not. Somewhere, centuries off, he heard his own voice ask: "Am I dead, then?" and the old man answer: "We shall see."

His head was warm. The Park was grand in the spring.

"You will sleep, and perhaps later you will wake. Now, calm."

The old man fluttered, a white bird. His robes against the snow, bare feet in the ice. On top of the mountain, the blackbird's eye, the old man in league with the sun. He was a blackbird now, his robes the iridescent soot of their wings.

Off the cross he flew.

Calmly he watched himself rise, curling like smoke, serpentine with ancientness. He joined with the old man and they began to twist around each other in a macabre tarantella toward the sun. Below him, a boy under a tree; above him, the emptiest eye.

Gone.

Then: whiteness.

Somewhere a voice was chanting. "Do not be afraid," it said. "We are both pilgrims here."

CHAPTER 5

NALDJORPA

"Still. You must remain still if you are to get well."

The voice was the voice of the old man, nearby. Soft and even, it stated a matter of fact, neither imploring nor commanding. Firm slender hands removed a bandage at the side of the young man's head, dabbed on a mixture of snow and herbs, replaced the dressing. The hands moved down his body slowly, probing the back of his neck, caressing the wrists and chest and ankles, while the voice was a hum of odd syllables halfway between singing and prayer.

Grey was the shade, and pain: pain had returned. Not the shirt of fire now, but that overall insistent queasiness Jed had experienced last when, laid up for a week with the flu, a ten-year-old boy who still believed in Hell begged forgiveness and release from an unseen confessor. His body was beyond him. It existed out there somewhere. Concentration, desire, despair: nothing could induce his renegade limbs to obey him, and he hovered, immobile with fear, on the border between fearing he would die and fearing he would not.

He and Will, another evening. A dance he recalled; a dance, and then the club, and too many tonics and gin. The first year of prep that had been; he was sixteen, unused to mixtures. Most of the night his mother had sat with him, forgetting her own creeping illness to

78

console her intemperate, retching son. Afraid he was at first, afraid he would not make it. Then, as the last of the evening's hors d'oeuvres tumbled out from between his jaws and the spasms of heaving began, his concern shifted, and he became afraid that he would not, after all, be permitted to die: that this moment of gastric and mental chaos was to be, as promised by the scriptures, endless.

Through the grey wash, lights. Dimly aware of cool pressure at his temples, Jed tried to rise. The lights danced. But there was nothing to see. He pushed himself up a fraction of an inch with his elbows, and the greyness swirled. This time he knew he had moved, for the lights were suddenly within him: a million small flames, they teased and poked him back down.

His entire body was stomach. He was hungry beyond any recollection, and yet the idea of eating was horrifying. Besides, there was no way he could feed himself, no way he could rise, no way he could do anything but slowly, laboriously, breathe.

As degrading as the sensation was to him, it had the virtue of familiarity. A down coverlet, music in the parlor, and his mother's hands tinkling china. Ten he had been, and thought he would die. He had got through that one. Now? The lights were a network of stars, and he wanted to vomit again. He clenched his fists weakly; a dull pain ran up his arms.

I can feel, then, he thought. Yes, this was somehow familiar, he had done it before. Again he strained to push himself up.

"You will only hurt yourself, young one. Be still. Later we will talk."

Hands pushed him back and Jed fell gladly, happy for an excuse to surrender. His mouth opened and he struggled to form a question, but before the cracked lips had mastered a syllable, the soft voice had responded.

"Tibet, my friend. You have endured much pain. Rest, now."

The resonant mumbling began again, and Jed lay back to listen and to rest. Throughout India he had encountered holy men who chanted in this way, but the old man's voice was unlike theirs, the style sparser and more insistent; somehow, without a note of urgency ever creeping into the chant, Jed understood that the syllables were a specific petition for his welfare.

He had made it, then. Through what miracle of chance or design, he could not say. This was Tibet, and feeling was returning.

Rest. Yes, the old man was right. He had been through as much as a boy could take and still return. He would rest, and entrust himself to the ministrations of this gentle stranger. He closed his eyes, and the lights danced brighter. The chanting continued, and a crackling of wood. The scent of cedar, then dark.

While his patient slept the old man busied himself about the fire, replenishing the spent cedar branches. Chanting almost inaudibly all the while, he melted snow in a small brass pot and dropped into it herbs from a string of small pouches dangling from his neck. He stirred the steaming mixture with a stick and, each hour, soaked a new bandage for the boy's wounds. After each changing, he arranged the folds of his robe around him, sat crosslegged in the snow, and shut his eyes. The strange sounds continued.

When Jed awoke there was a new fragrance in the air. Mornings, and he a child again. The rich nuttiness of roasted grain. His nostrils sucked in the new aroma greedily.

The grey was beginning to clear. Above him the lights separated, merged, took form. Slowly he opened his eyes, and the shifting greys came together to make shapes. Depth and coherence returned, as out of the confusion of blurs a single image congealed.

Slate or silver it was. Three sides. A triangle, a lance-head.

Squinting against the first brightness his eyes had had to endure in days, Jed sought to make sense of the figure. Then it nodded and he knew what it was. A beard. He forced a small smile and moved his eyes above it to where the old man's eyes, steady as this unexpected dawn, were fixed on him.

"You have slept long, young one. You are almost late for breakfast."

Jed blinked slowly, once, twice, and stretched the muscles of his face gingerly wide, easing himself cautiously out of he did not know how many days of coma. He breathed eagerly at the mix of cedar and grain, then sniffed and shook his head as the wood-smoke bit his eyes. He was warm on his back beneath a canopy of some rough fabric, a tan cloud between trees. He raised himself on wobbly elbows to inspect his rescuer.

The old man was stirring the brass pot over a small fire. The heat of the fire had melted a circle of snow an armslength around it, and within this enclosure of ground he squatted, clad in a *dhoti* and sandals. The canopy, Jed surmised, must be his robe; he had exposed himself to the winds to shelter his sleeping charge. For a moment Jed watched him work at the food, wondering what manner of man it was who would surrender his only garment to a stranger to provide him the amenity of a windless sleep; then he remembered this was Tibet, where humans and demons and gods were cut from the same cloth. He smiled with the recognition that in this land of desolate mysteries he could accept as perfectly normal the apparent comfort of this old man half-naked in the snow.

"I am grateful," he said.

"There is no need," came the even reply. "It is I who should be grateful."

He turned and came toward Jed, the steaming pot in his hands. "Here," he said. "You must take very little at a time, for you have not eaten in three days, and your body wishes to return to you, but slowly."

Jed allowed himself to be propped up against one of the cedar trees that supported the canopy, and took the hot metal shakily between his hands. He forced them to hold on to it as a charge of warmth coursed through his limbs; then he placed it in the snow beside him and breathed deeply of the fumes. Squatting in the snow beside him, the man produced a slice of bark which he offered to Jed as a scoop. He dipped this into the gruel and brought it to his lips eagerly, lapping at the unknown mixture until it ran down his chin and his wrists and into his mouth.

Tsampa. The porters had eaten a coarser version of it which they enhanced by the addition of yak butter, generally rancid, and tea. This was purer, simpler— roasted barley boiled in snow—and it evoked in the wakening patient the recollection of wheatcakes and syrup, his mother at the piano, those ancient Saturday mornings.

As fast as the heat would allow he shoveled the watery gruel into him, slowing as he became full and the old man's expression of guarded concern turned gradually to one of simple satisfaction.

"I am glad you enjoy it," he said taking the empty pot from Jed's hands. "It is all we shall eat for many days."

Jed accepted this pronouncement with equanimity, receiving with deep satisfaction the unspoken implication that his destiny was now linked, for what indeterminate future, to that of this aged apparition who had nursed him from the pit back to health. It was a time, his ordeal past, to let someone else take charge. "How long," he asked hoarsely, "have I been out?"

"Out?"

The grey eyes danced merry as the meaning of the idiom sunk in. "I do not know. It is two days since I came upon you. Before that?" He shrugged.

The eyes narrowed, inspecting the head wound at a distance while the slender hands rinsed the brass pot with snow. "Your head. It burns still?"

Jed nodded, cautiously, then held his head still as the man's hand reached toward him and came to rest just above the left temple.

Instantly the fire was gone; his head felt as if it were being bathed in a rush of mountain water. He drew back, startled, but the man's eyes offered no threat, and he allowed him to keep his hand on the wound until fire and water alike had passed.

"You are strong," said the man. "Strong in body, strong in *chi*. Many would be dead now, but you are strong. The head will trouble you for a few days, but we will keep the poultice on, and it will heal. Now," he finished with mild apology, "you must walk."

A firm hand clasped his wrist, pulled him abruptly to his feet. For a second he thought he would black out, as the blood of three day's recumbency fell in a rush to his feet. Foggily he grabbed the man's arm for support, and the moment passed. Then, with labored and aching steps, he allowed his guardian to walk him twice around the fire and back to the tree.

"Enough. Later today, three times around. Tomorrow, a dozen. In two days, you will run."

Jed accepted the instructions without comment. It was comforting to surrender the immediate future to another will.

All that day he lay beneath the tree. At nightfall,

feeling his strength returning, Jed offered the old man his robe.

"You need the shelter and I do not, young one. Keep the robe."

The response was kind but firm, and so Jed slept beneath the flapping cloth while the stranger sat beside the fire, his thin legs crossed, spine straight and eyes closed, as comfortable as far as the boy could make out as if he had been wrapped in ermine. The following morning broke shrill with a vulture's cry. Jed sat up tense, alert to danger, as all the horrors of his two days on the plain flooded back to him with the sound of that harsh clarion.

The old man was not at the fire. Jed's eyes ranged rapidly in a circle. Nothing but ice, brush, and rock. It occurred to him that even though for two days this rude camp had been his home, it was in fact no closer to civilization than the cairn against which he had almost died, and that without the man who had dragged him unconscious from there to here, he was in little better shape now than he had been then. What if his rescuer should not return? What if he became lost, or was attacked by bears or wolves? Quickly Jed pulled himself to his feet. Reborn, fear tapped at his spine.

But that would be too much. Caprice could not extend so far. He sat down, leaned against the tree. He was angry at himself for having given in to such easy terror once again. Something the mountain had shown him. Had he lost it already? He closed his eyes, breathing cedar. Salt pinched his eyes as he forced his mind to concentrate.

Images of the slaughtered porters, of his father's head rent from the shoulders, of the black-toothed captain streaming blood, swam through an uneasy brain. He pushed them aside, imagined nothing, imagined himself already dead, imagined—the mountain.

He could not say how long he sat there or how many times his vagrant thoughts forced him to review the events of the last several days. The sun was high when he heard shuffling in the brush beyond the camp, and he opened his eyes half expecting the bear, the demon Cyclops, or Blacktooth.

The old man was observing him from just beyond the fire. In his arms was a bundle of twigs. The sadness in his face was mild, unastonished; Jed was convinced there was no use pretending anything to him, that he would have to admit to this strange solitary his hope, and his despair. He had betrayed his own vision, and the man knew. Suddenly, with all the penned terror out, he began crying, furious, unchecked; his screaming rivaled the vulture's cry.

The man set the firewood down and walked slowly to his patient. "It is time," he said, "for us to speak."

His name, he said, was Naldjorpa. For the next several hours Jed talked and he listened in grave, attentive silence. Occasionally he would interrupt the narrative to clarify some point obscured by the young man's grief and distraction, but for the better part of the afternoon the Tibetan hills echoed only the pained and faltering voice of the pilgrim who had been through death and who now, rescued as accidently as he had been first imperiled, sought a meaning to the ordeal.

As he wove his tale of slaughter and gold, Naldjorpa was mute beside him, casting twigs to keep the fire up, nodding, drawing the teller out of his pain. From time to time he would close his eyes for long minutes, yet Jed retained the impression even then of an alert, sympathetic intelligence. Toward dusk, as Jed was speaking of the gold, the hermit assumed a meditative posture. Quite slowly his eyelids rose and his gaze fell full on the speaker.

"The gold," he whispered, and the trees hissed with the solemnity. "What gold is it of which you speak?"

"It is," Jed began, "a type of gold peculiar, I gather, to the Himalayas, to Tibet. A kind of white gold, I think. My father knew it better than I, but it was, I believe, the finest color I have ever seen in a piece of jewelry."

"A piece of jewelry." The old man's face was impassive.

"The medallion. The Arab's medallion." For a second Jed considered that, during one of his intermittent meditations, Naldjorpa might have missed this important part of the tale. But no. The man was on a different tack entirely.

"Yes," he said. "You have spoken of the medallion. It is the medallion that brings you to Tibet. It is medallions that most seek here. It is the medallion that has taken your father's life. But it is not the medallion of which we are speaking."

The grey eyes twitched into a smile, and for a second Jed perceived at their centers twin points of a red brilliance. Behind Dhaulagiri the sun was beginning to fall. As their attention moved together to the mountain, Jed realized what the old man was getting at.

"Yes," he responded with sad illumination, "there was that gold too."

"The mountain's name," he breathed, "is Dhaulagiri. The people of this region believe it is a holy mountain. They believe that if a person climbs to the top of Dhaulagiri, he will see God."

"I have heard that story," Jed nodded, "in Kathmandu."

"And what do you say of it?"

"I don't know." The tone was glum, resigned. "Last night, last week, I thought . . ."

As the boy's voice trailed off Naldjorpa laid a hand on his shoulder.

"You are saddened," he said, "because you have lost the gold. But I will ask you again: of which gold are we speaking?"

"You are right," Jed acknowledged. "The medallion is a small matter. The gold of the mountain, though . . . For a few moments back there, for a few moments before you arrived, I thought I had . . . I had . . . that," he finished quickly, "my death was a small thing, and not to be feared."

"And now?"

The young man's head shook. He sighed once, deeply. "Now it is gone."

"Listen," said Naldjorpa. "This is the highest place in Tibet. From here all the waters descend. Each spring the snow of these mountains melts and fills the small streams, and they run to the rivers, and the rivers run to the seas. But at the top of the mountain, there—"

His arm swung wide and, in a grand fluid gesture, aimed at Dhaulagiri.

"There, there is no melting and no running down to the sea. On the highest peaks of these mountains the snow has not melted since men and women have come to the valleys. The snow has been there since the time of the gods and demons, and it will be there when you and I and all our children have joined your father as food for birds. That highest ice is called eternal; the people here call it, because it does not die, precious. The precious snow.

"When once you have seen it, truly seen it," he finished solemnly, "it is within you, and cannot be lost."

"And yet," Jed whispered, "I have lost it. I can say, yes, this I saw, and that. But in my heart I do not have the feeling any longer. In my heart I do not want to die, in my heart I am afraid."

"Dying," said Naldjorpa, "is the easiest thing in the world. It is living that is difficult."

"But to be beyond it! To be beyond your own death, and still alive! I thought, when I awoke here, that a gift had been granted me. And now I feel cheated, humiliated, as if my father's death and my own illumination was a trick played by some caprice, some evil mind. For a moment I thought . . ."

"Tell me, then, what you saw."

Jed talked again, piecing together for the old man as much as he could recall of his last several hours on the cairn. His blindness, and how it had passed at the dawn. The gold at the peak of the mountain, and the explosion; the carnival of demons, and the murders, and drinking from his father's skull; how the mountain glowed again and how, for one thin astonishing instant, he had known that he and it were one. All of it he recounted with a mixture of exhilaration and sadness and anger, anger at its being, now, forever lost. When he began to tell how he had started to imagine himself already dead, Naldjorpa stopped him.

"That, I believe, is the moment I had the fortune to find you."

Hesitantly Jed nodded. "Yes."

"At first you were grateful. Now you are not so sure."

A slight annoyance at his perceptiveness jostled Jed's defenses, threw up his ego again.

"Yes," he said again, quietly.

"Well," the hermit continued, "is it not fitting that you feel bitter toward the man who dragged you down from the mountain?"

"I do not doubt your kindness."

Naldjorpa smiled skeptically. "There is kindness and there is kindness. Perhaps you would prefer to be dead?"

The young man's head shot right, sought out mockery, but there was no edge to the question.

"Not that," he replied. "No. I only mean that after this the rest of my life looks a little . . . pale, perhaps."

"Hah!"

Jed had not expected such heartiness from one so serene. He smiled, embarrassed.

"How can you say what the rest of your life will be?"

Jed bowed with swift ceremony. "I must find a purpose," he said. "Something to explain why this has happened to me. Why I am here, left alive. I will stay in Tibet."

"Until you find the gold?"

They smiled together.

"Until I find the gold."

Gradually the bones got stronger. A week, was it, a month? Jed had lost track of time. Since the slaughter, nothing had been real. He was not yet prepared to say what the hermit was. No one, he thought, no one in his right mind, would choose to live in these mountains. Yet who was to call this madness?

They talked as Jed's body knit. Neither was communicative at this juncture in their lives, and so they contented themselves with celebrating the sparse beauties of the landscape. Naldjorpa showed Jed how to find herbs under snow, how to obtain sustenance from chewing certain barks, how to catch fish through the ice with a yakhair line and gold hook. He felt, for a time he could not count, an appreciative child again.

He walked each day a little more. Naldjorpa was insistent, and after a short space of lethargic frustration with the necessity, Jed came to see how important it was, and came to enjoy it. He was getting stronger, the air was thin and crisp; he was starting to feel some of the first rushes of purely physical exhilaration that a young athlete feels when he knows his body is finally in shape. That such an ordeal should have had this consequence tickled his sense of proportion.

One day Naldjorpa came to him before dusk. The winds had been bad that day, and Jed was still cold. The old man leaned toward him, his hair a haze in the firelight. In his hand was a bowl of *tsampa*. "Soon," he said, "we must leave. You need food now, not bark."

Jed wondered that, up until now, he had been—what, reluctant?—to ask this extraordinary man about his life. A shudder of apprehension, and then he faced him.

"How are you able to survive out here?"

The smile, and: "It is not a mystery. A concentration of energy, that is all. There are many here who do so. Some lamas give performances, in the villages below. It is an exercise. You will learn it easily."

"I?"

"You have won against the snows this time. But that is only one battle, and you are not beyond it yet. When you are well, we will speak again of concentration."

Jed spoke hesitantly. "Are you to be my teacher?"

"You have much to learn. And apparently," his grey hair a dance to the caprice, "a providence, yours or mine, has given me the task."

"Who are you?"

"I am Naldjorpa. A pilgrim."

"There are other monks here who go about unclothed like you?"

"I am not a monk."

"Who, then? Who, if you are no priest?"

Shrugging, the comical flash of a slapstick clown. The steel eyes merry. "I am, again, Naldjorpa. I live here."

"And what," Jed eased out, "do you do?"

That cackling glee, the sun in his eyes. "Do? The

West is a strange country, my friend." Then, sudden ancient sadness, the smile of the whimpering buddha, and directly: "I gather firewood, I cook, I eat, I shit and urinate, sleep and meditate—what you I believe would call yoga."

"To what purpose?"

A slice of impatience wrinkled the old man's features, passed. The answer was clean.

"To see God, of course. For what purpose were you seeking gold?"

A chide, Jed supposed, but let it pass: he had little invested at this point in maintaining an illusion of his own pure intentions. There was an *I Ching* line which spoke of deception: It is no use making false pretences to God. The sense of the observation rocked him as never before. He knew he could not lie to this man. For the rest, a modest curiosity:

"You belong, then, to no monastery? No order, no disciples or friends?"

A chuckle, a jolly old elf: "I do not have followers. As for friends, the mountains send me what I need when the time is right. That is why you are here."

Jed could accept that. He felt certain that the appearance of the hermit two minutes short of his death could not have been merely accidental, but pointed to a vast, undisclosed appropriateness: he felt not simply that he had been saved, but that this man particularly had been sent to do the saving, and that he had been saved not capriciously, but for a reason. And conversely, as Naldjorpa was implying, that he himself had been sent, by what forces no one yet could say, to fulfill a portion of the hermit's destiny. They were met.

And yet he could not escape the fact that this was no contest of equals, that there was something extraordinary about this man.

If man he be.

No! No more mumbo-jumbo, he vowed. If this man were something other, something more, then the Parousia was at hand, and Jed had fallen into bliss. The fact that the old man should welcome the unexpected intrusion into his isolation flattered his sense of importance as much as it gratified his sense that in this universe which looked so insubstantial, nothing in fact was by chance. But he knew he must allow the peculiar wisdom of this time to unfold in whatever form it chose.

"I had the impression," he said, probing, "that you glowed as you came down the mountain, as if you and the fire were one. A kind of halo . . ."

"As I came down the mountain?" Naldjorpa interrupted.

Jed nodded. "And across the stream."

"The stream, yes."

"You came down the mountain and walked across the water and to me."

The smile an easy capitulation, the shrug of the one to whom winning and losing are the same.

"As you wish."

But Jed could not let it lie. "You did, didn't you? You did! I saw you! Floating, shimmering down the mountainside, across the stream. Then I blacked out, I guess."

"Close," he murmured. "So close."

"Tell me: what did I see?"

Naldjorpa sniffed. "I do not know what you saw. Only you know what you saw. In the moments before the body drops away, the eyes are able to see many things they cannot see when we are awake, or asleep, or dreaming. In those few moments, much is possible."

"I saw you glow," said Jed, defiantly. "A cloud of light."

The smile was comradely, affectionate. "You are familiar," he asked, "with chemistry?"

Jed nodded, glum, expectant.

"Bodies of matter, as you know, give off electrical vibrations. All bodies do, that stone's as well as yours and mine. These, in contact with the atmosphere, produce chemical reactions which make the vibrations visible to certain observers. This light you in the West call *aura*. Everyone has this aura, though only a few perceive it. You are among that few."

Not in his life before had Jed ever been conscious of any special ability in detecting light emanating from bodies. There had been that psychologist James, but his evidence had been no more than hearsay, and Jed had written him off as a crackpot.

That seemed now a far land. This was Tibet, and all things seemed possible.

"Do you mean," he quavered, "that my seeing you within a halo was an illusion?"

"Not at all. What you saw was energy, energy in a form you were not used to. You will grow used to it here."

"And the mountain? I saw you float down, walk on water."

"As you wish," he shrugged again, his amiability infectious. "At the doorway of death, many chinks in the cavern are opened. As for the water, however . . ."

He lay a hand flat on the ground, lifted it with mock ceremony and pressed it to Jed's cheek.

"Anyone can walk across a river in winter. Only the young fox must beware."

Indignation checked, unresolved. "Is it nothing but tricks of the mind? Have I imagined it all?"

"Of course you imagined it. As we imagine our life. As we imagine it, so it is."

"But did it really happen?"

"Why do you ask me this? Is it not you who should know?"

"But I do not know!"

The shout a cry of hurting, a deep-gouged hatred, desperate. "Help me," softly, "please."

Naldjorpa's firm hands on his shoulders, a grip to bruise and awaken. "Listen," he said. "What do you prefer? That I am a man, a god, or something else?"

"I just want to know," said Jed crying, "what has been happening to me."

"And so you will, young one. Where do you wish to begin?"

"I know I must stay in Tibet."

The old man's twinkling eyes. It seemed his entire face opened, reached to embrace the chill air. "Tibet," he said, "is large. And you can no longer stay here. A week, and our food will be gone. Animals there are to kill, but I do not favor that."

He stopped, as if musing. Jed felt the need of apology, yearned to repay this grey stranger his life. Soon, he sensed, they would be leaving the mountains —how far would Naldjorpa stay by him?

"I am strong. I can travel now."

"You are strong, yes. Rest, then: one day more. To-morrow we will leave for the valleys."

"Valleys?" So long they have lived in the ice, he had forgotten that elsewhere the planet was green. "Which valley?" he asked.

Naldjorpa pivoted, spread out his chest. The smile a second dawn.

"East," he said.

CHAPTER 6

WHITE DREAMS

For the next three days it was ice. So high had they been into the mountains that two full days of walking —and the old man no slacker—were required to bring them within sight of the plain. The constant motion invigorated the young man even while it caused him considerable discomfort: Naldjorpa had apparently decided that Jed was not to be coddled any longer, and set a pace that wrenched and juggled every bone of his still recuperating frame. Jed bore it well, confident that this extra ordeal served some as yet unrevealed purpose, and gradually noted that the pain, being constant, could more easily be ignored than one broken intermittently by comfort. It was a burden he could bear.

They walked from dawn to midday, stopping only occasionally to rest, and then for no more than a few minutes. At midday, a bowl of *tsampa* each, and some talk—generally less than Jed hoped for, for Naldjorpa could not be accused of garrulousness. They continued then until just before dusk, when Naldjorpa would call a halt and they would take another meal and then sleep. It was a grueling, monotonous routine, suited, Jed imagined, to repair.

And to thought. The swirling white set him often to contemplation, and he found his mind turning obsessively to the ambush. He squirmed at the recognition that the pain of his mother's death had been wiped out at last only by the horror of his father's murder.

Cross-bound again, he tried to shake the recollection by concentrating on the landscape. It did not erase the new pain, but it helped.

Nature had provided the Tibetan plateau with little in the way of pictorial variety. It was not the kind of country, Jed noted wryly, you would be likely to find on a postcard. The noise of the winds would have made speaking difficult even if Naldjorpa had been so inclined; and the vastness of the stretches of ice filled Jed anew each morning with a sense of dread majesty. Maybe on the open sea, or on the Western plains, he had felt this isolation; he was sure there were few spots on the face of the planet so overwhelming in amorphous intent as this windswept Himalayan plateau. The mere flatness of it jolted him, awoke him to the possibilities of space, and made him realize what confinement he had hitherto accepted as normal.

Jed could understand why the people of this plateau held the mountains in a kind of religious esteem. The Harvard neopragmatist recoiled from the notion of human beings worshipping stone, yet he would be a liar not to admit that the sight of these sheer, glistening peaks never failed to shudder his spine, make him gasp for coolness. They were simply the single most impressive creations the earth had performed. As Dhaulagiri retreated to the West, other, equally startling, forms made their appearance, passed, and were gone. The march of the mountains on either side of them as they made their way down the valley between—it was the grandest spectacle he had seen.

Gradually, against that constant, impassive presence he began to doubt the credibility of his senses, began to wonder whether in fact this had not all been a whisk of his mind. The slaughter was real, all right. Real, too, that he had nearly died. But this old man, and the bear, the eye, the skull . . . ?

The mountains he could see. They were palpable, and no less exhilarating for that. The hermit ahead he could see. Himself, too, amid the swirling snows. But the thoughts that had come before death, the visions of his own slaughter and release, these he now doubted, as the understandably lurid pigmentation of the last minutes of breath. Dreams. No more.

On the morning of the third day Jed woke to the smell of *tsampa* on the fire.

"You are tired, young one, but the morning is gone. And there is something you should see."

Sheepishly Jed tumbled himself up, shook his eyes awake, and accepted the bowl of steaming gruel. The sun had sliced halfway down the mountains to the north; they were a white frieze between greys.

"Is there nothing in the mountains but ice?"

Naldjorpa smiled. "You are impatient to be 'somewhere.' That is understandable. But that is why you must get up. What I have to show you is there."

He swung out his arm in that magnificent gesture, as if he were lord of all of this. Jed followed the sweep of his arm out to where, at the eastern horizon, a thin streak of brown hovered in the midst of the white.

"What is it?"

"The border. The edge of the ice. Food, other pilgrims, warmth."

"A village?"

"You could say that. Though people are nomads here, and so not as settled as that."

Jed scooped in the *tsampa* gratefully and gazed, confused, at the brown streak. They would be there tonight, perhaps, at the rate they had been travelling. He did not understand why the thought was less than cheering.

One would have thought he would welcome it heartily, the notion of imminent companionship. Yet his mind, grown accustomed to privation and the arduous pace of their journey, had not been prepared for so speedy an end to this leg of his ordeal. He had, in fact, begun to relax into the strain, and was not at all sure he was ready just yet to throw in with villagers—nomads or otherwise.

They might, however, he reminded himself, have news of the bandits. Might even have seen them. Reason enough, he supposed, to go.

"We will get there today?"

Naldjorpa nodded. "Tonight, perhaps. We will walk as you wish today, so it is up to you when we arrive. One thing, however . . ."

The last steaming scoopful of grain. A swish of snow for the bowl.

"That," Naldjorpa pointed to the empty bowl, "is the last of our food."

They came out of the ice at dusk. The first knots of returning hunger had just begun to pull at the young man's stomach when, several hundred yards distant, the brown streak dissolved, congealed, took form. Squinting against darkfall, Jed made out a circle of huts, each of them also a circle, around a central fire. Yaks grazed in a loosely rectangular corral some yards off, and a single sentinel stood shadowy, between them and the camp. The figure made no sign, either of greeting or of admonition, as they approached.

The humor of the situation hit him. Penniless, four miles above the sea, companion to this extraordinary outcast . . . his rating, as Will would say, was not high. If this were America, and the camp below Sioux or Shoshoni, he would be shaking with anticipation, wondering whether the savagery within would prove to be bloodthirsty or noble. Here in Tibet, he did not know what to think. Scarfer had said something about Tibetan hospitality—a mark of honor among them, was that it? A fact unquestioned, a given as integral to the mores of this plateau as was suspicion to the people of his own climate.

And yet: what had he to go on? Two of the natives he knew well. One had orphaned him; the other had saved his life. He felt as much at sea as if this were Montana.

Abruptly Naldjorpa stopped. "Go to him with the begging bowl," he said quietly. "It is the custom."

Briefly Jed brightened, realizing that in spite of the old man's disavowals, this simple injunction bound him, however tenuously, to discipleship. Grimly through the haze of memory he grabbed at kinship with the hundreds of novices he had seen in the streets of Calcutta, begging for their gurus. Through the dancing of pride with despair, he acknowledged the sweetness of being led. A spark of knowing, shackles dropped, and he embraced for the clear moment devotion, and freedom. For that instant he understood the peculiar wisdom of which Alec had spoken in praise and in awe of the Goliards: that wisdom, despised in the West since the Renaissance, that identified itself, without regret, with poverty. In New York the two of them would be objects of pity and scorn; here, among the immense ancientness of the snows, Naldjorpa, he was sure, would be an honored guest; for the East had not yet begun to confuse material success with understanding. For a moment this knowledge held him, and he smiled at his guide and rubbed a finger lightly around the inside of the bowl.

But the past was not yet worn. He had never begged before. His few contacts with beggars had been as a wealthy American vacationer; he had given freely, generously, with little thought to the recipients of his largess. Now, to be the recipient himself of another person's charity—the idea was a little repugnant. All he had been taught before this journey had suggested that the beggars of the world had, by some unseen cosmic design, met their own level. Darwin modified by Will's mentor William Graham Sumner had provided the essential justification of the division between classes, and if his parents' wryly skeptical approach to the theories of the social Darwinists had served to mitigate the zeal with which the young man received their argument, still the essential message had been well digested: in the natural order of things, it is the strong —and the rich—who survive.

This, however, was Tibet. The "natural" order was reversed. A man to whom he would have thrown dimes in New York had killed the last of his family; and Jed himself, scion of the ancient and reputable house of Dey, was reduced to a staff and a bowl.

He confessed his uneasiness to his guide.

"I am not surprised," said Naldjorpa. "The West is skilled at taking. A few among you learn how to give. But to receive . . . that is the hardest of tasks. Because you have had a great deal, you have not had to learn to be thankful."

"But," protested the boy, "it is not that I am not grateful. For all you have done, I am most—"

"I was not speaking," Naldjorpa cut in, "of myself. I do not require your thanks. It is the people below that I mean. They will give without your asking, for that is the way of this land. It is not your thanks they are seeking, but only that you return their kindness, should the occasion ever arise, with a kindness of your own."

"I will do my best."

"I believe you will."

In the event it was not so bad. Jed remarked how

rapidly he was able to justify the unusual activity to himself when the impulse for its execution proceeded not from a social theory but from his stomach. By the time they reached the settlement it was nearly dark, and Jed proceeded bravely, undaunted by the ghosts of his past, into the small enclosure of tents. Thoughts of marauding savages subside, the pilgrim becomes the clear soul, when a man is hungry. They had not eaten, he guessed, in twelve or fifteen hours: Naldjorpa seemed to have been unaffected by the fast, but Jed had been. Swimming, rather than walking, he had been for the last hour: the sight of the Indian village, nested in the hollow of these hills, had struck him, by this time, as a godsend.

In the face of his hunger even his wariness of people subsided. He found himself, as in a wanly pixilated dream, moving into the tiny encampment with delirious abstract glee. Simon Girty, coming home. For an elevating moment, he knew they would welcome them both without restraint. A smattering of fancy, a passage through veils: for that moment he was swept out of time. It was 1876. He had just been born. Born into a village like this one, some continents removed, and a papoose, he hung on a tree. His mother stirring grain, his father daubing paint for war. The amazement, the air.

And he, now grown, was hungry. Bowl in hand, and staff, he entered the Indian circle. Behind him Naldjorpa kept distance, allowing Jed the necessary danger to draw him out of his diffidence, when suddenly, before him—

For the briefest of shrieks, it was Blacktooth. Then, the vision passing, a man. Short, tight-limbed, his face grey in the first light of stars. Dressed lightly in skins, his arms bare, knotted, and lean. He looked quizzically at the young man bounding into his camp with a begging bowl at his side, then leaned on a shepherd's staff and waited.

Jed held the bowl out in his left hand, touched it with his right forefinger brought the finger to his mouth, and looked eagerly at the herdsman.

For a few moments, nothing.

Then, the Mongol features crackling, the brightest of grins, and: *"Manger?"*

Jed smiled, unknowing, and beckoned to Naldjorpa: they were received.

That the herdsman had spoken to him in French was a happy mystery until Jed recalled a little of the history of Tibet.

He and his father had talked of it coming up from Kathmandu. In 1897 Tibet was all but a closed country to the white world. The capital city, Lhasa, was still referred to, in the scattered reports that adventurers and naturalists had been able to deliver to the West, as the Forbidden City, so difficult of access was that holy place to the nonbeliever. At a time when Western interests had forced China to open its doors after centuries of seclusion, and when the Indian Ocean was archly thought of, even by Indians, as a British lake, Tibet—protected by the harshest geography on earth—had succeeded in keeping out all but the occasional traveller in search of loot or mystery. As a result Tibet had retained its culture intact, and among the bands of wandering herders who comprised the bulk of its population, there were only a handful who had ever seen a white face before.

It had not, however, always been so. From the seventeenth century on, the nations of Christendom, avidly murdering each other in their own backyards for the sake of this or that interpretation of the Word, were also sending emissaries abroad to lay the foundations for similar struggles in other peoples' lands. Chief among these spreaders of truth, Jed recalled, had been the friars and teachers of his own heritage: the French Capuchin and Jesuit priests who, by the middle of the eighteenth century, had succeeded in establishing a string of missions along the valleys of the Himalayas as fervid for Christ as were those along the St. Lawrence half a world away.

At first the Tibetans, unlike the heathen of North America, had welcomed these new establishments with the openhanded generosity dictated by their particular brand of Buddhism and which, it might fairly be said, was a kind of national sensibility among them. Even the high lamas and Lhasa saw no threat to their way of life in allowing a few dozen French priests to reside among their people, and so for centuries the cross had stood firm amid groves of temple banners and prayer flags.

But then the climate changed. Not content to exist with the Tibetans as equals, the Europeans began to push for dominion. The Buddhist religion, said the priests, was no revelation but an error; the lamas spoke without proper authority; Chenrezig, the beloved patron of Tibet, was no true saint but an imposter.

Why the French clerics felt that, after so many decades of peaceful coexistence, they could succeed in unilaterally changing the terms of the gentlemen's agreement that kept them in Tibet—that question, perhaps, may be consigned to the student of religious psychology. In any case the outcome was inevitable. Summary orders were handed down from Lhasa that this traitorous talk cease. The French, who had been willing if need be to die for their faith, would have none of it, and so, within a matter of weeks, they were escorted politely to the border and their small missions, with some exceptions, razed to the ground. In a century of labor for the Lord, the Europeans had succeeded only in antagonizing a nation and leaving to posterity, amid the myriad mounds of prayer stones that already dotted the Tibetan landscape, a few spent memorials.

And—Jed nodded a silent thanks for the ironies of history—a few speakers of French. A few untutored herdsmen, perhaps one or two in a village, whose grandparents had seen the Europeans come and go and who recalled, from tales around the fire, snatches of an exotic tongue that were, in this year of advancing grace, the sole mementos of the abortive Christian incursion.

That, at any rate, was Jed's speculation. He had little chance to test his theory, for little more than the essentials of communication had survived the centuries, and his attempts to engage the herdsmen in conversation were met only with genial nods and stares of general incomprehension.

Food he understood, though, and sleep; and with the assistance of Naldjorpa, who spoke the local tongue, the two were soon bulging with rancid *tsampa* and bedded down, comfortably exhausted, in one of the skin tents. The villagers were, if mute, most generous. Jed slept deep that night, and for the first time in many days, without dreams.

They stayed in the village five days. Jed became increasingly conscious in this brief passage of time how thoroughly his mind had gone over to the blandishments of a simple, rural existence. As he helped Ganmor—his host, the sentinel of the first evening—drive in yaks at evening, as he ran races with the boys of the village and watched the children laughing at Naldjorpa's tall tales, especially as he allowed gongs and shawm to lull him asleep at night, he became even more aware of the remoteness of New York, the seeming insignificance of that whole former span of his life.

After a week his inner clock had ceased to run, and

he moved lightly, as in a listless dream, from one sunrise to another.

He could not, however, forget the bandits. Naldjorpa had come upon him, some days after their arrival in the village, quizzing Gan-mor: had anyone seen, he was asking, a group of four horsemen, one with a single blackened tooth? *"Dents, dents!"* the herdsman had nodded gleefully, but beyond the recognition of the French word Jed could get no information out of him. A flurry of staccato monosyllables, and Naldjorpa turned to his charge.

"No, he says. No one has seen these men."

A blend of elation and disappointment, and Jed nodded his thanks.

"Young one," the old man had said.

"Yes?"

"This eats upon your mind. Your body is strong now. Do not trade one weakness for another."

"Do you mean," bristled Jed, the code of the West on the rise, "I should forget about it?"

A smile of compassion, then: "Forget? No. That is not possible. But the world is wide, and you have other matters to consider. Sometimes," and the grey eyes lowered sadly, "such a thing will take care of itself."

Jed had fallen silent, let the brooding subside. He would let it sit, yes, because he had no choice. In the city perhaps. Traders, the marketplace, crossroads: he would let it sit, but not die.

He drifted in to the calm rhythm of the village. By day there was work, and he lent it all the support of his recuperating body. At night there were stories—which Naldjorpa patiently translated for him—and *chang:* under the gentle influence of this harsh barley beer, Jed would sit for hours, fascinated by tales of demons cooked up for the delectation of the young by the old men and women of the camp. Tibet, he discovered, had

105

a very rich demonology: for a land as fully dedicated to its religion as this one, the priests had concocted a pantheon rich and varied enough to satisfy all sensibilities. Boddhisattvas there were, in numbers both kind and terrible. Female adepts as well, who functioned not only as consorts for the gods, but as goddesses and *herukas* in their own right. And a host of bestial apparitions, half man and half bear, progeny of the monkey and ogress who by legend had spawned the people of the plateau—the full phantasmagoric panoply he had imagined before only in dream.

It struck him that, for all their chatter about the horrors of the wild, for all their inventions of the monsters so dear to childhood, the villagers were a people remarkably free of fear. The tortures of the damned, in which the young ex-Catholic had been so strenuously versed, seemed to have little place in their myths.

There was of course the anxiety about wild beasts—including the most horrific of that breed, the hidden marauder Yeti—that one would expect from a people living on the fringe of a vast and hungry wilderness. There was, too, a more amorphous anxiety about conduct, about acting and feeling and speaking well to one's fellows. This was not, to be sure, equivalent either in origin or effect to the West's fascination with sin, but simply that high level of concern for the common weal that one would take for granted in a small, closely knit group of fellow believers: an unkind word, it seemed to be the general idea, was to be frowned upon not because it endangered the soul of the speaker but because it made the life of the community at large—which included the speaker—that much more arduous. And there was—again on a level so reduced as to be foreign to a mind raised on the notion of the importance of personal comfort—some concern for food, shelter, warmth.

But of the peculiar horror of personal death, of the general horror of death itself as a brooding abstract stretched over the whole of human consciousness—of these poignant Western ideas Jed found very little evidence. The fears of the Tibetans were immediate and circumscribed. Death would come to each of them, to be sure: but some rude pragmatism had convinced them that worry over this particular inevitability was a misplacement, a waste, of energy. They accepted the notion of mortality with an equanimity that Jed, hardly released yet from the labyrinth of questions that had racked him since the massacre, found refreshing and, inevitably, more confusing still.

One thing had brought it home to him.

It was the third or fourth day they were there. Crying awoke him. He pushed aside the flaps of the tent and strode into the sunlight. Milling groups of villagers, mist steaming up to the mountains, and off to the side, a circle of people, hovering, expectant. For that morning, as Jed slept, a child had been born.

Within the knot of admirers were parents, grandparents, friends. The child, still streaming blood of delivery, howled erratic into the grey morning of the steppes. The mother, already up, leaned over; the father, bent against a staff, grinned toothless, chuckling, swigging *chang*. Jed rubbed his eyes, stretched. It would be a good morning, he told himself.

From a tent on the edge of the camp came an old woman holding aloft an image, still wet, of Tara, the Tibetan mother of compassion; behind her walked a young man holding a knife. They walked loose, somber, to the circle of admirers.

Jed was unaware, half awake. In dim recognition he watched the old woman approach the knot of wellwishers, watched her take the infant in her arms and carry it, the young man in train, toward the river.

Without a sound he saw her unwrap the pink, scream-ing bundle, hoist it up by the ankles, plunge it quick, one two, into the icy water.

No! his education leapt. And a hand, firm with com-fort on his arm, saying: wait; this is not your country.

They dragged the baby out. Whimpering came only from the family. The old woman was silent; close, warm, slow, she worked on the gasping figure. Caress-ing, rocking, humming low. More blankets are brought, fires stoked; by now all the village is up, and the air is full of the smoky, plaintive voice of chanting. The old woman leans over the child. Her mouth goes to the tiny lips. She breathes. Around her the family waits.

Nothing.

More blankets are brought. Closer the old woman leans. The mother's cries increase.

Beside him a firmer hand. Rattled, shaking his head in unbelief, Jed felt to his right a hand tight, unyield-ing, calm—the hand of his master and friend.

"It is," said Naldjorpa, "a custom. In a harsh land, the customs are harsh."

"Will the baby survive?" he asked, tremulous.

"Who can say?"

Eyes back, taut, to the scene. Over the bundle, the woman. Behind her the man, the family. From the child, no sound. Jed: flash of potential, quick rise, make it to the wall, scale it, saber out. Take these heathen down.

Then, beyond. In the flicking of an eye, beyond the hope of the Samaritan and the, he knew, more indul-gent hope of the Brahmin, to—what?

Jed could not say when it was he knew he could not rescue the child. Somewhere between the recognition that he was not capable of receiving this cup and the recognition that it was, after all, not his business, a shaft of resignation bit. This was, finally, Tibet. Not his country. What mysterious designs, what fearful symmetries, they chose to perform here—was it any of his concern?

Whimpering, the mother. Brave against laughter, the *chang*. The old woman took the baby, shaking, and rocked it, singing low. A cry, a shudder, and: done.

Beyond the circle the people began a chant. Pulled from the hills they began the rich and raucous keen of the Buddhist devotee.

How long had the child been alive? An hour? Three? Bleak, desolate, the acid of despair eating the windings of his brain, Jed cried. Why? asked his Jesuitical mind.

"Because," said the greybeard beside him, "it is a harsh, harsh country."

He turned, salt tearing the edges of his eyes. Naldjorpa's mouth was a bitter grin: for a moment he saw in the old man's eyes the recognition, the acceptance of all the suffering, all the uncertainty, all the misery of this round. Not absolution. Not the impossible practice of Hosannah, Hosannah in spite of what horrors moved here, but acceptance, nonetheless.

They took the little body down to the river. Without ceremony, without wonder or despair, the mother took the stiffening form from the old woman, laid it on the bank of the river, and stepped back. A moment's courteous farewell, and the young man stepped up. The knife at his side, the father restrained by friends. The tiny form, blue already in the impossible Tibetan cold, motionless on the bank of the stream.

The dissection was simple, quick. One flash for the head, one for the legs together, one more each for the arms: within a minute the child that had breathed its first breath before sunrise was fit only for prey. Stilted, moving with exaggerated ceremony, the man took the severed limbs in his hands, one by one, and strewed them over the plain, where they would make food for vultures and bears.

The keening chant went on.

Naldjorpa's hand on his arm, Jed fought back explosion. Twenty yards away, the mother and father of the infant held each other, shuddering against the Himalayan morning. The old woman who had performed the ritual shuffled off, swaying with what sympathy only her forebears knew, toward the tent on the edge of the encampment. The young man, red trailing the blade, followed.

"Death," Naldjorpa said to him, "is neither horrible nor joyful to us. It is hard, only, and inevitable: like birth, something that must be gone through."

"But do you not, do these people not, fear what might happen afterwards?"

"Afterwards?" The old man's eyes danced.

"I mean . . ."

"You mean Hell."

A nod, silent. Finger in the flame, eternity minus eternity equals eternity. Yes, he admitted.

"Hell," explained the old man, "comes in many forms. We do not take it in the form that is popular in your country. The idea of a place of eternal torture, where the wicked go after they die—that has not taken very strong roots here. Some of your priests tried it. It did not work. I cannot say why that is so: perhaps as a people we are simply not inclined to be unhappy."

The twinkle of the sequestered mage. As if, Jed grinned, a people could be doomed to this or that sensibility. For the Tibetans, an arduous life, a brief death, acceptance. For his own people, long life, long death, worry.

Jed searched the crinkles of memory for that long ago drunken episode on the Charles. He and Alec: was there a life after death? The words were lost, adrift.

110

Something, however, about rebirth. He phrased the question carefully.

"Is it not easier for you that you believe in reincarnation?"

The old man's face a genial blank.

"Reincarnation?"

Spluttering, flustered. "Yes. I understood, I thought, that the Hindu faith, the Buddhist faith, taught that the soul migrated from body to body. That death was only a spot on a greater line, and the soul would be reborn into another body . . ."

His voice trailed off in question. He searched the old mans' face.

"I am not," he said, "one of the faithful."

Jed listened. Little the hermit could say would have shocked him now, and the discovery, if that it was, that Naldjorpa subscribed, by his own admission, to neither of the major faiths which Jed had just offered him brought him only a momentary distaste for the intricacies of dialectic. He knew he was far from the end of his search, and at this point in the journey he was willing to forego easy conclusions, ascribe special wisdoms to systems other than his own, if only because his own had thus far given him so little satisfaction.

"What," he asked quietly, "are you?"

The laughter a rush of delight. "You need more *chang,* my friend. If I say: I am Madras University, 1821—will you believe me? If I say: yes, I am a Hindu, yes, I am the Buddha, yes, I am the Nazarene—will you believe? Each one is only a road, young one. I am for the snows. You must find your own way."

A momentary release. A flicker of recognition. Sniggering, was it, or wisdom: yes, the old man was right, he needed more *chang.* Then:

"I would like to stay with you awhile."

The breaking of Eastern dawns. Almost a child, this greybeard. But:

"No, it is not yet time. Tomorrow, these people will move. We will help them, you and I. Then, they will go north, into the plain, to seek fresh grasses and water. You and I must go a different way."

His arm again, in that sweep to encompass the world. This time, east.

"That way," he said, "is Lhasa. One week's walk. I am to bring you as far as the city gates. Then we must part ways. For a little while, perhaps. Later, we will talk again."

The simplicity of the absolution appalled Jed. "Do you mean," he quavered, "I will not be seeing you for . . . for . . . ?"

"Time," said Naldjorpa, "is a game we play. All people play by different rules. We have known each other for how long now? A month, two months, three? What is that? You, young one," and his grey eyes steeled down, affectionate in a way Jed had not seen before, "are more important than that."

"I do not understand."

"No," said the smile, and breathed: deep, the mountains involved. "No, you do not understand. But you will. Tomorrow, the road. They to the north, we to the east. In two weeks, Chakpori, in Lhasa. You will find friends there, and medicine. Still, now. On the road we will talk again."

A week later, they looked out over the valley from the crest of a ridge. Grey, but with hints of green, the valley stretched down, winding, sharp in the prenoon sun, to where two rises of rock breasted their way up from the river. On each one, a castle.

The one to the left, massive and elegant as only the

productions of aristocracy may be. Seven stories, countless levels and windows surged toward heaven, stately and brilliant. The topmost floor, Jed noted, was painted a dramatic red, and over the rest of the valley this scarlet sentinel swept its imposing, ubiquitous glance as if it had been so ordained by powers here before humans.

"That is the Potala," said Naldjorpa. "Within live a thousand monks. In the upper stories are the Dalai Lama and his retinue."

The hill to the right supported a smaller but no less imposing edifice. Its beige walls seemed to grow naturally out of the side of the rise; around its fortified walls, a display of prayer flags fluttered in the late March breeze.

"To the right," said his guide, "is Chakpori. That is where you must go. They will not refuse you entrance."

"I?" asked Jed, tremulous. He had forgotten momentarily that this was to be his last day with the man.

"When will I see you again?"

The hermit smiled. "Who can say?" he replied. "The paths of the living are winding, they cross not once but many times. My time in the mountains is not yet done. When the time is right, we will meet again. Now," he said, kindness caressing the boy's pain, "it is time for you to go."

"Yes," he nodded, dumb. Yes. It was still a day's walk to the valley, and storm clouds were swirling above.

"Thank you," he whispered, "for my life."

The old man was turning to go. No ceremony, then. The notion pleased him, since he was able to convince himself that a parting without banners and speeches would less likely be final than another. A quick smile, then, a raising of the palm, and goodbye. Jed watched, salt licking the corners of his eyes, as the hermit picked his way back toward the ice. When he had gone a few yards, however, he turned. Wind whipped his hair, but his voice was the sound of spring.

"I am thankful as well. One thing I leave with you."

He breathed, acknowledging the early thaw, and his grey eyes met Jed's. There was a gentility there the boy found irresistible. The man was bathed in green.

"Are you sure," he said, "that you have not already died?"

In the moment it took Jed to absorb what he had heard, Naldjorpa was gone.

Above him the castle loomed rude, handsome. The silver haze of moonlight suffused the roadway into a cloud of expectation. No birdsound broke the deadness of the night, no wind rattled the arcane clarity of this fog. Jed walked suspended, his feet light for the first time in days, touching laurel and mistletoe and rock as he worked his way up the hill: touching them with a hesitant reverence, gently, as if to draw their manna at a pass.

As I was stone, so now the tree.

Scruff foliage passed him on either side; the rock path climbed. He was gusted now, but strong from weeks (or months?) on the trail; another power than his own seemed to have him in hand. I am an actor in a play, he said aloud. I am a bird on the wing. Chuckling: the image of Alec and lute. That empty vastness gone. Would he ever see Will or Jenny again?

Before, the castle darkening. The storm was coming up fast.

It was perhaps a hundred, two hundred yards, to the gate. Within, warmth, a bed, friends. And yet, this last small league, he did not know if he could make it. To come so far from the emptiness of the plain, and then fail . . .

114

Spring near, he mocked himself. Bunyan's most terrible truth. In the last hour, as angels are near, then you fall. This must be March, he thought: how deft the divine irony, to send a storm not a mile from home.

The wind was rising fast now. A wall of wind before him, it made each step a conquest. The beige fortress greying as the sun died behind him, he watched the adumbrated paleness of his own image stretch plaintively before him, as if, he himself lost to the task, the shadow at least would home before night.

No. He couldn't make it. The wind was blowing hard now, pelting him with stones. He hunched into the tattered parka, tightening his eyes against the mountain's attack and gripping his hands into fists inside his pockets. It was bitterly cold, but he would ride that out gladly if only he could be rid of the wind. No Nor'easter this: the chill dry winds of Tibet seemed to deny gravity itself.

He could not see twenty yards in front. The castle was a mirage, the road a shifting of sands.

The sound of engines rose.

To the right, just off the path, a rock ledge jutted out the length of a body. Beneath it, a hinting of brown. If he could not make the castle, Jed thought, he could make the rock. And there he could wait out the night.

From the wake he had never been born, Jed groped now for the light. Stonewind flailing, a yellow biting fog. Around him shadows of slaughter, terror, goldlust. The wind was a howling worse than that of the plain. He bucked against it, straining for breath, but it was no use. The wind drove him down, and he felt his hands, unseen, scrape ice. Vast clouds marched behind the castle as he gave in to the storm.

Gradually he dipped beneath the torrent; gradually, painlessly, he gave in to the howling, let the dust drive him down.

On his knees, again. The snow a blessing amid the torrent. Jed licked at it, smirked, and began to crawl toward the rock.

Beyond imagining, this the glacier too. No castle before him, but snowgold. No hope or help from pain. "A lesson once learned and forgot—must be learned again." The inexorable pressure of the past, that wayward leeward dragline, that is the grounding of all your life and the cause of its pleasure and pain. How escape, and yet remain whole . . .

Until, suddenly, he was there. Under the overhang Jed pushed deepening troughs of white away from him. The earth was bare; only a few patches of ice disturbed the rough brown surface. He breathed a thanks to what ailing gods were left him and began to pack the snow up around him in a small hemisphere. In a few moments he had constructed an inexpert but serviceable ice hut. Not an igloo, exactly, he smiled: more a child's fort. But it would get him through the night.

He leaned against the inner wall of the makeshift cave and stared out into the storm. A white whirling, no more. Shrill, a madness of machines: somewhere a siren, somewhere a body dying.

He was not afraid yet. A few hours these storms lasted. Even if it kept up through the night he could make it. The snow wall encircling him was high enough to keep out all but the most insistent winds, and he caught himself a moment sniggering at his fortune, as if he had stolen a march on the storm. It was not warm, certainly, but he had been cold before. It shut out the yelling wind. And it was dry.

Outside the last rays of sunset, faint though they may be, would be piercing the snowshield. Somewhere. From where he sat, the entire world could be white.

Many a night he had spent with Naldjorpa in caves, through storms as bad. This hut, bolstering ice against ice, would see him through. He gave a brief humorous nod to French pragmatism. He was hungry, and tired, but alive.

Wolf's hour, sometime before dawn, the whirling outside subsided. Had he slept? He did not know. Before him the wall had climbed higher than his head, and now it nearly touched the overhang above him. Shell of the egg, closing on the unborn. Behind him the rock and his spine were one bone. Beneath him the chill of the earth had ceased to matter. He could not see out the cave.

Abandoned, then. Abandoned and immured. He could die here tonight and it would be weeks before full thaw would erase the tomb and reveal his stiffened body to curious monks. They could be passing outside this minute, unaware that the mound of white hunched up under the familiar ledge concealed a human being not yet succumbed to the ice.

An ant, a worm, lice on a mastiff's coat, had more reality now than he did. Here he could expire without waking, and no one to say he had passed here, no one to carry his bizarre history home. It was at once terrifying and immensely funny, this notion of lives on either side of a wall. Outside his chamber it was, perhaps, daylight. Monks coming and going, gongsounds welcoming the sunrise, travellers and traders scuffing the stones two feet from where he sat, and not one of them suspecting what the ice hut contained.

He would die here, then, two feet from morning. Weeks later they would discover the body. They would purse lips, shake shaven heads in wonder at what the sunshine brings. He would be carried off and gilded, as one of the enlightened, as a gift of the capricious snows. In the end he would become a god.

Had not his entire life been like this? Unseen, unfathomed . . . he had been entombed a long while, and only now saw it so. Within the frozen security of this cave, he stared, mutely terrified, at a white wall; beyond that shield, beyond that paper-thin, impenetrable barrier, a vast profusion of consciousness, millions of eons of living and dying beings, went about their business unknowing. And he, prisoner of the ice, a teeming profusion himself, locked here against eternity as surely as each of them, in their own tight minds, were locked.

We are all, he smiled, prisoners of thought; he, perhaps, was more clearly a victim than others, yet all carried crosses and all were buried alive. His own calm astonished him. Interment, it turned out, was not the horror it had been said to be. When he was a child, he recalled, Poe's "Cask of Amontillado" had kept him up nights on end, staring frenzied at the ceiling of his bedroom chamber, imagining the unthinkable: that this was no bedroom but a tomb, and never again would the door open. He would remain here until the skin hung tentlike on the bones, until the flesh rotted away and the bones themselves, pulverized by time, were nothing but a puff of grey against the sheets.

No wonder, he grinned, he had run screaming into the arms of the Church.

But now? No, it was not unbearable. Perhaps, as Naldjorpa had said, he had already died, and this was but a replaying of the most ancient of tales. Once again, stiffened beyond hope or fear, he was to await the end walled and silenced against the light.

He could break out, dash this wall down with a single shove of his boot, yet some perverse attraction for the purity of his dilemma prevented him from moving. He took cheer knowing that the monks outside were unconscious of his presence, that presence which was finally their own as well. The silent teacher, he nodded self-satisfaction and remained still.

And what was beyond the wall? Only a life he had

known already too long. The rules of that life tired him, he would be free of the rigid design even at the cost of his breath. Smugly he felt the joke to be not on himself but on them.

The thinking, at last, was faulty. Was not all thinking faulty? Was it not all chimera: him here immured, they "outside" living the dream—Naldjorpa, even, in the snows? Was his father less real now his body was gone? Was the son less so, unseen? Perhaps he was already dead.

Terror turned to pity; pity to disgust; and then, almost too close: skullgrin.

There was, at the end of things, no wall; the wall, too, was a lie.

Have you thought you might already be dead?

Naldjorpa's farewell now pressed him easily, steadily, into the rock. By the time they found him, he grinned, he would be but a dream of the earth.

At a moment: no inside, no out.

And the wall beginning to melt.

The storm, he now knew, had passed. The howling outside had subsided, and he sensed, as if through egg-shell, the first faint flush of morning seep into his cave. Suddenly he breathed deep and smiled: it was all right, he thought, to have made it this far. If he had been willing to die, why then: why not be willing to live? Down from the glacier, with rare delight he watched the snow run in colorless rivulets down the wall opening his eyes to the dawn.

Beyond the chink of his cavern, a face. Peering down at him with restrained curiosity, quizzical, bemused, and yet not at all surprised. The features were Mongolian, but gaunter, more angular, than those of Gan-mor's people. High cheekbones and an extremely narrow nose were the most remarkable elements of a small, shaven head; from out of a copper cloud a pair of tiny black pupils danced happily, and thin lips parted to reveal a row of even teeth, spread in easy delight. He was about Jed's age, and he stood slightly favoring his left side. As Jed unfixed his limbs and began to push down the wall, he continued staring, with that remarkable absence of either suspicion or awe, as if travellers quite commonly made their appearance at Chakpori in just this manner.

The flash of another lifetime. Jed raised himself, accepting the young monk's helping hand, and in that moment Jonathan and David were met: some twitch about the eyes, a wrinkle of embryo, a blink, told Jed that somewhere not on this planet, not in this age, he had known this man before.

"I am Tobsan Chen-la." The voice was unaccented, fluid. "And you," he said nonchalantly, "are expected."

CHAPTER 7

SCARFER

"Yank, eh? Don't get too many yanks through here. The climate, you see, the mountains. Ruddy British'll hoof it to Peking you give 'em the papers through, but the yanks, now they sit tight in Calcutta for the most part, sipping Bombay gin. Lovely country, America. Everything a body could want, I hear tell, streets of gold. Why, I was reading in the newspaper only the other day, some university blokes, they was doing a study, and you know what they found out, guv? America has got the richest urine in the world. God's truth."

Will did not like this man. It was not only his vagrant dress, the stink of his outlandish hair, or the way his Cockney syntax seemed to transform even his occasional decorous remarks into the rankest of vulgarisms. Will had seen beggars enough in Calcutta not to be offended by the personal debasements that clung to India's poor like the inevitable flies about a carcass. He could forgive even the fact that the shabby figure across the table was a white man, and so culpable as the natives were not for his flagrant insouciance in dress and speech. Even though he asked more of his own race than others, he was conscious he did not know the man's history, and it might well be that his present condition of defilement was not entirely his own doing. Will was not ungenerous.

No, it was not the shabbiness itself that offended him, but the easy familiarity with which the stranger had come up to him here on the streets of Kathmandu—the assumption of brotherhood, of shared intentions, that seemed to underlay his entire manner of approach. The man seemed to think that, simply because he was a Westerner, they must have something in common.

Not that his appearance, even without this extra annoyance, would have disposed Will to welcome his companionship. Sandals clad his feet, which were black with the road's debris. Loose muslin trousers and an elaborately tooled felt vest were his only garments of clothing. At his waist, a leather pouch slung low off his hips. Around his neck hung a string of amber beads, in the center of which a shell medallion struck as he gestured against a hairless, sun-browned chest. His black hair streamed from the crown of a small, bony head, and every inch of skin carried a patina of dust.

His eyes were deep; black or brown, Will could not tell, but dark, piercing, alive: they danced about his face erratic, as if he were afraid to focus on anything. He spoke in a grating tubercular whisper, smiling as if all of his life were a lark. He was vaguely menacing and entirely self-contained. Will did not like him at all.

But he was, it seemed, the traveller's one link to his friend.

"Jethro? The good Jethro? Of course. Sit you down, pilgrim, and Scarfer will tell you a tale."

That had been this morning. Wandering as near his wits' end as he had been since leaving Paris, Will had stopped for a cup of tea in a café, and there had been buttonholed almost immediately by the disheveled Cockney.

"Scarfer's the name, guv," he had rasped. "Think I might be of some help to you."

Will, noting with displeasure that the man did not

122

wait to be invited to sit, had asked, "What do you mean?"

"Hear you've been hunting yanks. Had no luck at the mission, can tell that by looking at you. Might have better fortune with me."

It was true he had had no luck at the mission. No luck in fact since Paris. Gloomily he recalled the laborious past six months. Madame Blin had very possibly led him down the garden path. From Paris to Le Havre, from Le Havre through the Mediterranean to Suez, then down the Red Sea, across the Arabian, around Ceylon, north through the Bay of Bengal to Calcutta. Twelve thousand miles of merciless sun, seasickness, and boredom.

Then, overland, by porter and camel and a sacrifice of comfort that made the sea voyage look plush by comparison, to Nepal. Six weeks more of adventureless, sizzling ennui, with none but Asians to talk to, no chance of a bath or a decent smoke, and scant hope that, once he got there, Jed would be anywhere found.

He had grown hardy on the road. Worked his way through exposure and dysentery and exhaustion, and he was, he knew, a better man for it. It was the single light in this whole blasted affair. Now, finally at Kathmandu, where the Frenchwoman had assured him answers would be available—nothing. Last evening he had arrived, and gone straight to the small Protestant mission, the one place he knew could be counted on for civilized conversation, a good scrubbing, and—if the Deys had passed here at all—word of his friends' whereabouts.

But no. The aged minister who ran the mission for the spiritual welfare of the few dozen Nepalese who deigned to drop in for soup and prayer had known nothing.

"Americans, you say? I'm British myself, you see.

We see very few Americans this way. Can't say, sorry, that I've seen your friends. You'll stay the night, of course."

Will had stayed and, this morning, his belly full of Episcopalian cant, had ventured into the bazaar to see if he could pick up anything. The people will be talking still, Mme. Blin had assured him. Well, there was damn little truck with the people; not one in twenty even understood the meaning of the phrase "white men."

By noon he knew he could count on scant assistance here. So, he supposed, he should be thankful for Scarfer. What eccentric providence had sent him the traveller's way, Will could not guess; had he had a say in it, he would have chosen a less abrasive guide. But earnest at least he did seem, and in any case there was nobody else.

"Coupla jars for me and me friend," Scarfer muttered to the Bengali waiter. Then, to Will:

"Now you're a friend of Jethro, you say?"

Will hoped his blinking did not make him seem too much the ingenue to this creature. But: Jethro! He ignored the intimacy. It was far more than he had hoped for. He unbuttoned his jacket.

"I am. I am, indeed. You know him?"

"Let us say, guv, we've spent some time together. How long you been after him now?"

"I've been trying to find him—him and his father, that is—for nearly six months. They've been away for over a year, and we fear . . . well, let that go. How is it, may I ask, you know his name?"

Scarfer smiled, revealing bad teeth. "Ah, your friend Jethro and me, we've 'ad our share of piss-ups, you see? The odd jar, the occasional ginger. Quite a drinker, your friend. Can't say the same for his da."

Will was stunned. "Both of them, then? Both alive? You saw them, spoke to them? Here?"

"Easy now, guv. Six months it's been, and I'd not be wanting to raise your wishes too high. But, yes: last I saw of them, they was both kicking and hale."

The beers had come, and Will placed some coins on the table. The waiter was instantly gone. Scarfer raised the froth to his mouth and drew. "Nothing," he exclaimed, "like Nepalese *chang!* Do you in in a dot."

Will sipped the pungent brew, replacing the glass and looking close at his guest. "When did you say you saw them last?"

Scarfer calculated ostentatiously on his fingers. "Musta been," he mused, "before the biggest snows. November, maybe, or December. You've got to understand, guv: time out here ain't what it is back in the States."

November. Yes. That would be about right. Will figured the approximate travel time, added some weeks on for accident, and yes. His distrust of this man made him elaborately cautious, yet in search of his best friend caution was not superfluous. "I asked at the mission," he said. "The priest there said he had heard nothing of Americans here, nothing for three or four years."

Scarfer took another draw, all but draining the glass. "The vicar?" His voice was lightly contemptuous. "The vicar wouldn't know an American if it came up and bit him in the arse. Barmy, he is, know what I mean? Too much of the juice, too many years down the pipes. A good sort, he is, but no Cook's Tour, if you see what I mean. Have another, guv?"

Will waved away the offer, pushed his glass across the table. "He is, you mean, not sound?"

"Sound? Yah, that's a good one, guv, never heard that one before. Addled, yes. Barmy, crackers, a bit over the eight. Good sort, though," he finished, slugging Will's beer.

The minister had not seemed so to Will. A bit idiosyncratic perhaps, with his chatter about the green fields of home, his insistence on grace both before and after the meal, his difficulty in recalling Will's name even after the young man had repeated it twice. But that was to be expected of an Episcopalian. He was far from sure that the old man had been mad.

How far could he trust this grey stranger? How much did he really know?

"Do you recall," he asked with guarded deliberation, "where the two were bound—and to what purpose?"

Gleeful cackle, half the glass gone. The eyes, zeroing him down. "Tell me, guvnor, tell me straight like. Would you be testing me, now? Nah, never you mind. I know how you feel for your friend, I don't blame your wondering about me, truly I don't. Perhaps this'll set your mind at ease about whether I know your man or not."

He reached into the pouch at his waist and withdrew something wrapped in cloth. Meticulously he undid the folds of the packet to reveal a silver-cased pocket watch.

"Go ahead, then, take a look."

Will picked the watch up gingerly and turned it once, slowly, in his hand. His expression softened, then became tight. "Yes, it's Jed's. I don't suppose you'd care to explain how it came to be in your possession?"

"A gift, guv. One bloke to another, you might say, over beers. In a kind of payment, you see, for services rendered."

"Jed loved this watch. He wouldn't give it up to . . . what services did you render, may I ask?"

"Why, porters, guv, that's all. Him and his da, you see, was near as eager as you are to be off. It fell to me to make the arrangements."

"And he gave you this in payment?"

"They'd had some trouble, guv. Thought the solution might lie north of here."

"Solution . . . ?"

"Call it answer if you like. Where the prize lay, you see. The North was where they figured it would be. And what *it* is, you already know, no matter how dumb you play. What they were after, guv," draining the last of Will's beer, "it was gold."

He drew out the single syllable long, lascivious. Will felt suddenly threatened.

"Gold. That's right, guv. Something about a medal, a piece of jewelry, I ain't sure. I'm not one for trinkets myself. But your mate and his da, that they were. North they were going. Over the mountains, down the Brahmaputra, to the lamas. Where it comes from. The gold, I mean."

"Yes," Will nodded. "How long would the journey be?"

"For you," he said, "or for them?"

"What difference does that make?"

"The difference, guv, is that they made the journey in the snows. You'll be making it, if you make it at all, in the heat. Snow is likely to slow you down, so for them, two months, maybe three. For you—you look like a hardy lad—for you, with good porters, maybe one."

"And the destination?"

That raucous cackle again. "The destination, is it? That, my friend, would be up to you entirely. Why, you might not make it beyond the first pass. Plenty of villains out that way now. Might be in a dust-up and gone with you, then, before September is a day. Then again, you might make it through to Lhasa with no aggro at all."

"Villains, you say. What kind of villains?"

"Suresh! Another round for the guv and me! Villains,

you say? Why, villains would be plain or fancy villains, that's all. Bandits, you understand. The Wild West and like that, but you won't be able to hollar for no sheriff. The mountains are full of 'em now. We have here," he leaned over, that onerous winking again, "what you might call a social problem. The peelers go out time to time to round them up, but it's a rum trip. The hills are full of 'em. The government people can't round up but a handful at a time. There's a place, just beyond the mountains, they gather. A regular El Dorado for them villains. They hide out in the hills, ready to pounce, you see, and your traveller coming through peaceful like, and smash! they got him by the tail, and no folks at home is ever going to hear from him again."

He seemed to delight in the menace of the explanation. "Why don't the authorities do something?" asked Will.

"The authorities? The authorities, as you may have noticed, guv, have got enough to do here in town. What with collecting fees for prostitution and drunkenness and other crimes against nature, they hardly got the time to be running out into the hills to drag in bandits. They're only a trouble to nomads and the odd wayfarer like yourself. No, it ain't the authorities you'll be wanting. You get yourself some porters, see, and you buy 'em carbines. Then, when the villains are down on your band, why you just up and blow them to kingdom come."

The prospect was less than pleasing, yet Will understood the necessity of protection, and resolved to outfit his party, even at Scarfer's suggestion, as well as his funds would allow. "I suppose," he said slyly, "you might know where I can get in contact with some porters. And carbines."

"For a small fee, guv, of course."

"That goes without saying."

"Pen?"

Will produced one. Scarfer ran it through his fingers, then wiped it in vast deference across his grimy trousers. From the pouch he drew out a scrap of paper and scribbled an address and brief directions.

"There," he said, extending the pen and paper across the table. "Eight o'clock tonight. We'll work out the details."

Number 14, Red Ganja Street, was a small dingy anteroom containing, against one wall, a low under-stuffed sofa and, in the center of the space, a warped and wobbly table. A thin Indian print provided meager shelter from the street, and another, hanging skewed from a frieze of nails, covered a door in the rear wall. As Will entered, a flurry of cockroaches scattered to the corners of the room and waited. Since these insects were the only inhabitants, the young man checked the time—it was 8 P.M. exactly—and called out the name of his prospective guide.

There was no response, so he scuffed through the roaches to the back curtain, shifted it aside, and knocked. Silence and a spray of dust. He tried the knob and, discovering it firm, backed away, whacked dust from the sofa, and sat.

This was surely, he thought, the least hospitable section of a town not long to begin with on hospitality. Scarfer's directions had taken him down a series of narrow, filthy alleys whose gutters were populated with whole families of beggars nearly as wretched as those he had seen in Calcutta. Mothers of twelve clung to bony infants, their bellies distended by malnutrition. Boys and girls of four reached emaciated hands toward the passing stranger, grappled for coins.

Moaning and stench was everywhere. Everywhere too was The Look: that haunted look of wonder and hatred and awe that had greeted him in every alley from here to Calcutta, that had begun to eat into his brain, had begun to detach him in a way that quite unsettled him from New York.

It was a look, maybe, that told of things he did not want to see, here or in New York: a look of dedicated privation which, in spite of his queasiness, held a raw dignity that he could not help but admire. Although it offered him nothing but enmity, he was drawn to it, to its meanness perhaps, more strongly than he wanted to acknowledge.

Outside of Calcutta he had come upon a travelling minstrelsy. A bombast of discordance and disease; one of them had had leprosy, boils. What were they called? The Balis, the Bards, he could not remember. Could have used a bath, for certain, all of them. The child looked as if she hadn't eaten for a week.

"She's just thin, sahib."

In Madras, they said, the beggars starve their children so they will be more pitiful, hence plentiful, sights for the eyes of the giver. Will had never seen such poverty. It upset him. His natural kindness as well as his belief in Progress were offended by the display. Old women and old men side by side in the gutter, clinging to each other through shabby rags against the night air. Families of ten huddled against the rain, their only shelter a tarp strung between poles. Children of five hobbling on makeshift crutches, their limbs ravaged by hunger to uselessness.

And, at the base of every hill, corpses. Stinking some, burned others, the rest being torn apart by birds.

Why don't they go home? he had asked.

They are home, guv. They are home.

For Will to have discovered that the world was not thoroughly paved with gold, that there were people starving and freezing through some mismanagement of the design, would have been no great news. It was lack of propinquity to, rather than lack of awareness of, the hungry three-fourths of the earth that had accounted for his hitherto meager interest in the question of their welfare. He would vote for any reform bill on the floor. He'd once even thought about Bryan.

But to see it first hand, to understand that this was but a slice of the problem, and far more awful than the journals had told . . .

"The very poorest of them, sahib . . ."

India had meant nothing to him before. Unlike Harvard, his own alma mater had laid very little stress on traditions other than its own: as a consequence Will's knowledge of the East had been gleaned from Jed, who had studied it with that snappish Yarrowville fellow. He'd borrowed Jed's *Gita* once, but it had not grabbed his imagination, and he'd returned it practically unopened.

But now. This terrible poverty.

The worst of it returned:

In Calcutta. The poorest beggars, sahib, place cockroaches on their infant's eyes, then bind them fast with cloth so that, the insects having eaten out the pupils, the blinded children may be better objects of sympathy.

His stomach was queasy again at the thought. Something, he concluded, must be done. He would write a letter. Send a stipend. It pained and affronted him, this recognition that the Progress his schooling had promised was not in fact complete: that, far from being universal, it extended probably to no more than a fraction of the earth's inhabitants. For the rest, these screaming alleys, this lifetime of despair.

He hardly noticed the curtain part and his host walk in. In one hand Scarfer grasped a bottle, its alcoholic contents half gone. His voice rasped into the gloom.

"Well, guv. Hope you enjoyed your stroll."

Will rose not out of deference but in the hope of getting this business done with rapidly. "Is that meant to be a joke?"

A wave of puckish penitence suffused the Cockney's grimy features. "A joke? Oh no, guv. Meant no offence, to be sure. It's just that my friends here," gesturing vaguely outside, "don't get to see too many gentlemen down these parts, and so I know they'll have gotten a rise out of you, you see. Just wanted to be sure the transaction, as you might say, was not one-sided."

"I've given them what I could, if that's what you mean." Why did he have to put up with insults from this man?

"Ah, it wasn't the tinkle I was speaking of, guv. Just your being here is fine, if you take my meaning. Gives 'em a chance to see how their brothers and sisters across the sea are faring, you understand. Won't do for them to be getting no false ideas."

"Look, Mr. Scarfer, I don't mean to rush you, but I am in a hurry to be on. I've a hope to get to my friends before the snows begin again, and as you say it's at best a month of mountain trekking . . ."

Scarfer lowered the bottle from his lips and drew a wrist across his mouth. "Month at least, yes. And I wouldn't want to be holding you up no more. Just a formality or two, you see. Now you set yourself down there, I'll fetch my colleagues, and we'll have you fit out in no time."

He walked to the rear curtain, drew it aside, and knocked: a rapid series, five . . . three . . . five. The door opened, creaking inward. Scarfer turned and with elaborate flourish beckoned Will into the back room. Will followed.

Six young, somewhat squat female figures with dusky skin and enormous brown eyes hunched around a small square table, sipping something from metal cups. In the center of the table was an earthen pot. Against the walls candles flickered. As the two men entered, the group rose and nodded.

"These," said Scarfer, "are your porters."

Will shot a glance of unveiled displeasure at his host. "I don't understand."

Scarfer grasped, one in each hand, the two empty cups that had apparently awaited their arrival, and scooped out a murky brown liquid from the pot. "Not understand, guv? What's there to understand?"

Will, flustered, accepted the cup but did not drink. "But these are women!"

Scarfer's bad teeth caught the light of the candles. "And what women, guv! May they ever be blessed." Seven cups rose and halted just short of seven mouths.

"They're waiting on you, guv. Won't do to insult them, now. Some of these Nepalese lasses can be mighty stroppy when aroused—if you take my meaning."

Ignoring the innuendo with some difficulty, Will sipped the bitter liquid. Scarfer and the women followed suit.

"Now, what is it you don't understand?" Scarfer's voice was suddenly as mellow as the drink was acrid.

"Why, they can't be carrying heavy loads over those mountains. It's work for men, not women. Not girls like these," he amended.

"If you'll forgive the correction, guv, it's women like these who've been doing the labor of your travelling sahibs for centuries. Why, they're strong as any man! Kamala here," he pointed to the slightest of the brood, has been halfway up the side of Everest herself, more than one time. Don't you be fretting about this. It's the custom here. Why, everybody around here knows that: the best sherpas have always been women. And," he winked in that insufferably friendly manner, "they come

133

a bit less dear, I'll wager to that. You'd not be agin saving a pound or two, would you?"

"I am prepared to pay any reasonable price. But I prefer to have my packs carried by men. This is . . . well, this is positively impossible. We would never think of such a thing—"

"In America? Wouldn't you? Indeed? You'll have fourteen-year-old lads working in your mines, but you'll have no women carry bags? A curious thing, guv, and a toast to American gallantry."

Seven cups raised. Will screwed red eyes down. "I'll not drink to an insult."

"No offence, guv. No offence intended. Just reviewing the situation, if you see what I mean. You see, here in the East we do things a bit different. We do it simpler here. We give the bags to the ladies all right, and the children . . . why, we just let them starve."

He drained the cup.

"If you'll be wanting to get to your friend, mate, I suggest you do it my way. There's no one else in Kathmandu can get you porters like these for the price."

Again Will drank. The liquid seared this time, hit his gullet like stone.

"I suppose . . ."

"Sahib?"

It was the voice of the youngest girl.

"You are afraid we will drop the packs?"

"No, no, it's not that!" Will was conscious of a slight pressure in his chest, an excess of flourish to the hand that waved the question away. "I am not familiar with your ways. In my country it is the man who carries the bags."

"And the women? What do the women do?"

He explained, in as simple a manner as possible, that in his country, women were expected to do very little indeed. They were mothers, and wives, and were much esteemed for their generosity of spirit, the grace of their carriage, the purity of their souls. Kamala took this all in with wide eyes, then turned to her sisters and translated it into a rapid garble of Hindi.

They looked at him astonished. Will flushed, failed to protest as Scarfer refilled his cup.

"As I say, mates and sisters, to American gallantry."

Eight cups raised, eight drained. Will was starting to feel light. The idea of women porters offended him no less, yet for reasons beyond his understanding, the coherence of his protests was being washed out. The bitter liquid was unlike any drink he had ever had, and he was feeling light, conciliatory . . .

To his side Scarfer was beaming and, noticing this, Will straightened. "How is it that a white man is involved in this kind of business to begin with, may I ask?"

The cackle again.

"A white man, is it? Why, guv, they's no white man at all. Not white nor black am I, not toff nor wog. It's only me, you know, only Scarfer. And if anybody can find your Jethro, it's Scarfer."

Another cup down, another refill, and soon Will was drinking in challenge. Flushed as much by the idiosyncracy of the situation as by the floridness of the liquor, he felt curiously obliged to keep up with this offensive, weaving, petty entrepreneur. He held out his cup for another.

"If you have done him any harm . . ."

Scarfer raised an arm in mock defence. "The gods forbid, guv. We was mates, your friend and me. If you find him well, I'll thank you to send me the news."

For an instant Will thought he discerned in the darting eyes a screen of sadness, and on the basis of that instant he decided to risk the venture. The room was a maze now, and for one of the few times in his life he didn't care.

"How much, then?" he asked.

Scarfer smiled, refilling the cups.

"How much have you got?"

CHAPTER 8

CHELA

Chakpori was hard. For the several dozen *chelas,* or novices, who had elected to spend their youth at the Lhasa lamasery, the day began at four A.M. with chanting, small servings of *tsampa,* and study. Reading of the Tangyur, the major Tibetan scripture, and discussion of the life and labors of the buddha continued until nine, when a second meager meal was taken and exercise—in the form of yogic disciplines and menial labor—was conducted under the supervision of a master. Academic study was then taken up until past noon, when more *tsampa* and a short period of required rest gave the monks respite from the tedium of books and rules. The afternoon passed in much the same manner, but was more dreaded, since from one until past five the students were prohibited from leaving the classroom or in any way disturbing the concentration of others. This rule was enforced by canings and other forms of physical chastisement, and as the lamas in charge of discipline were not notorious for moderation, most of the student monks—many of whom had become chelas at six or seven years of age—carried bruises and welts as mementos of their occasional lapses of attention. From six until ten, more study, more chanting, more work; finally, at ten, sleep. At midnight the boys would be awakened for a brief service, and could then return to their pallets until four.

The harshness of the regimen was justified by the lamas on two counts.

First, it developed obedience and humility in a brood whose natural inclinations might well lead them into vagaries of indiscipline, discourtesy, and sloth. Obedience was highly prized by the Tibetans, both in and out of the cloister, and so the extreme rigidity of the monastic life was deemed not only justified but admirable. As for humility, it was perhaps the predominant Buddhist virtue, a goal to be striven for by lama and chela alike. Chenrezig himself, patron boddhisattva of the country, was known to have been among the most humble men —had he not vowed to forego entering nirvana until all sentient beings had been enlightened?—and the submission of his thirteenth reincarnation, the present Dalai Lama, to the rule of humility was famed throughout his land.

Second, the monastic way strengthened both body and mind to perform tasks that would have been considered impossible in a Western country. Concentration was the aim here. By concentrating the energy of the mind within certain prescribed disciplines, even the youngest of chelas was able to withstand the rigors of his chosen life with a remarkable degree of equanimity. The lamas over the centuries had perfected various devices to enhance the efficacy of their system of concentration, and it could be said that, if the severity of life at Chakpori was repugnant to a Western eye, it had achieved a number of minor miracles in the way of bodily control, breath regulation, and ability to withstand pain.

The virtues of passivity were well appreciated here. By concentrating on the One-Undivided-in-Itself, by surrendering the single ego to the whole, pupils were able to achieve an insensitivity to pain, a control over the autonomic nervous system itself, that would have astounded any Western doctor fortunate enough to observe their disciplines. The amazement that Jed had felt upon first seeing Naldjorpa unclothed in subzero weather was gradually mitigated here, since in Lhasa he witnessed many feats of like improbability. Firewalkers, fakirs pierced with knives, lamas who had survived prolonged interment—all were here in profusion. There were others, it was said, who could walk through walls, read minds, and fly.

It was not, however, these more obvious attractions that had convinced Jed to remain for a time in the monastery. Well before Naldjorpa had left him at the city gates, he had determined that, were an answer to be found to the question chafing him inside since the murder, that answer would be in Tibet. His sojourn in the nomads' village had confirmed his belief that, to justify his father's death and find a meaning to his own escape, he would have to undertake a radically different mode of life from that which had been his lot in New York. Something barer, harsher, more rigorous than that, was required—a way of life where death was not a question but a fact, where no anodynes were at hand and the seeker was forced to confront the issue of his own mortality each moment of his waking life.

For this the monastery seemed appropriate. The interest he had already begun to show in Eastern philosophies while at Harvard—the interest, it might be said, that accounted for his friendship with Alec—would here be satisfied and nurtured.

He was aware that all of Tibet was devout, and that much might be learned of the ways of these people and the paths to enlightenment simply by strolling through the bazaars of Lhasa and hiking the mountain trails from village to village. But he was in need, as Naldjorpa

139

had perceived, of more rigor than that: and so Chakpori, high on a hill in the middle of the city, had been chosen.

With his fondness for reading and study, Jed felt he would take easily to such a life, no matter how awful the toil. It would be, he imagined, like school—and he had always done well at school. The lamasery, as Naldjorpa must have known, seemed the perfect melding of contraries. The Harvard scholar's dispassionate curiosity could have full sway here, and the young man's lust for a more radical understanding of life, his yearning for acceptance, call it, or wisdom, or calm—why, that appetite was the very lifeblood of the place.

The presence of Tobsan, the young monk whose appearance had been his introduction to the lamasery, proved to be an unsought extra boon. He was approximately the same age as Jed himself—approximation being, among a people as lackadaisical about measurement as the Tibetans, the best that could be had in the way of determining a birthdate. His people, who lived near the Chinese border, were nomadic herders, but he had lived, he told Jed, at the Lhasa lamasery for over a decade, since he was nine.

That would have been, Jed calculated, around the time of the Haymarket executions. It both astonished and amused him that so many events he had at one time considered momentous, had shared over cognac and recrimination with Jenny and Alec and Will, had made no impact whatever on the life of this genial Mongol. He had been at tea dances when Tobsan came off the steppes; had been escorting Jenny to cotillions and arguing about the Gorman-Price Bill when Tobsan was first being caned here at Chakpori for sluggishness; and yet here they were, two strands of mystery twined, fellow sufferers on the roof of the world.

They had liked each other at once. Tobsan's ready

wit, his somewhat acerbic appreciation of the essential absurdity of most human beings' lives, had summoned up an immediate response in the young man whose recent brush with mortality had left him nearly as full of humor about his condition as of fear. This temperamental attraction had been supplemented by intellectual affinity; for Tobsan, an eager and imaginative student, had only recently returned from a two-year sojourn in Madras, where he had been sent by the lamas to acquire facility in the language and mores of the British. Thus personality and education combined to make the two *chelas* fast friends.

It was comforting to Jed, since he was the only foreigner at the lamasery, to have someone in whom to confide. One day at sunset, Tobsan found him staring West over the wall. "You are content here," he said, "but you have not yet escaped your past."

Jed smiled. "It's good for me here, I think. But it's over a year since I've been home, and I wonder sometime if I'll ever see New York again."

"Is it friends you miss, or the old ways?"

"A little of both, I guess. The ways of the mountains suit me, and I am getting beyond it, I'm sure. But sometimes I feel so . . ."

"Abandoned?"

Jed nodded with grim comprehension. "I had hoped they would come after me. Not that I would go back now, but just for the flattery of it. I'm far from melting into the One yet, I suppose."

"Pride is the last shackle, Jed. I know no more than four or five people who have ever laid it behind them."

"That's a comfort, isn't it?"

They smiled together this time, and Jed turned to a nearer pain. "Beyond it, maybe, is putting it too strongly. I do feel it hanging still, like a nightmare I haven't resolved."

Tobsan's response was gentle. "I wish I could give you a way to burn it out more quickly. But sometimes only time will do it. Do you still seek revenge?"

"Partly that, yes. Knowing that no one will ever pay for his murder. I hate to see justice so mocked."

"You know you can't say that. Whose justice? And do you know what will come tomorrow?"

"You're right, of course," Jed admitted. "But in the meantime, where do I go, what do I do? Until the great design unfolds, I mean."

Tobsan laughed—a broad, easy shattering of the mood.

"When I am tired, I sleep," he said. "When I am hungry, I eat."

And they laughed together again. "Naldjorpa told me," Jed said, "that everything is yoga. I'm anxious to know what that means."

"When he returns we will ask him."

But Naldjorpa did not return. Since the morning months before when he had left Jed, nothing had been heard from him, and from Tobsan, Jed could get only the meagerest information about the old man—yes, he knew him; yes, he lived up there in the snows; no, he did not know when he would return—until gradually Jed's eagerness to apply full attention to his studies overcame his fondness for recollection, and he stopped pumping his new friend for news. The hermit's name fell out of conversation, and only the image of the man, of those clear, wonderful eyes, stayed in his mind.

Patience, he was coming to learn, was nearly its own reward. The tedium of monastic routine, the lack of news from the "outside," the endless repetition of texts and tenets, the eternal sameness of life here in the East—all seemed to him part of an as yet unrevealed plan. When the time of the hermit was ripe, he would, as he promised, return.

Chakpori was not, however, all candles and hope. He had learned many practical things. Not only did he have the advantage of constant meditation—as he would have had at any of Lhasa's three monasteries—but he had also the specific advantages of acquaintance with Chakpori's specialty: medicine.

Since his mother's death Jed's mind had been turned, foggily and with some trepidation, toward medicine. Alec had had more than customary respect (considering his general inconoclasm) for its possibilities, and Jed had been quick to respond to his tutor's suggestion that perhaps the arts were not, after all, what he was cut out for. He was therefore, when his mother died, already strongly attracted to the science. Her death had clinched the interest. His third year at Harvard had included the usual liberal studies, but had contained two eccentricities. One was Alec's philosophy seminar, where he had been introduced to the *Gita*. The other was Anatomy I, where he had been surrounded by earnest Boston Brahmins eager to carry on family tradition by establishing lucrative general practices on Beacon Hill. The mettle of his classmates aside, however, the class had been instructive, and had whetted Jed's appetite for more. Could he had done this before, perhaps his mother would not have died. He nourished the hope that, someday, he would come upon a cure for the disease that had sent her to an early grave.

And here, in Tibet, behold! Accident or design, he did not care, had impelled him to this, and here he was, in the Tibetan version of the College of Surgeons.

The diagnostics were, to be sure, quite different. Primitive, some would say. But that was a Western bias; he rejected it, happily. While he was far yet from ascribing infallibility to the Tibetans, his experience as Naldjorpa's patient had convinced him that these people, whatever their backwardness by Harvard standards, were in possession of a medical knowledge as extensive, as specific, and as reliable as anything to be found in Harvey. Such suspicious ministries as herbs and massage played a large part in their counsels; yet Jed could not say, looking at his limited experience with these methods, that he had ever before in his life been more expertly handled than he had been with these people.

To his delight, elders of the monastery, perhaps on the recommendation of Naldjorpa or Tobsan, had seen fit to accept him not only as *chela* but also as a student of the particular brand of therapy for which Chakpori was famous: the study and manipulation of the aura. The halo of light that Jed had first observed around Naldjorpa as he himself hovered near death was the focus of Chakpori's investigation and its chief diagnostic tool.

However benighted his Harvard colleagues might have considered this system, Jed found it much to his liking. Apparently it was evident to the Chakpori masters that the young American had gifts beyond the norm for a person of his background, and they spared no effort, when once they had discovered his ability, in training and exercising his faculties so that the haphazard, fortuitous observation of aura he had experienced on the mountain might be transformed into a constant, general talent.

He had had, in this, some success. The ability to see an aura—a faculty which six months ago he would have dismissed as a charlatan's game—was, he came to understand, nothing inaccessible or arcane: it required some faith and a good deal of practice, that was all.

Assiduously he applied himself to the visualization exercises that lamaism had passed on through the generations, and within a few months, to his own considerable surprise, he found he was able to "see" illness in a person without even touching the person's body. Amid a gentle blue, for example, there would be splotches and furies of red: that denoted pain, discordance, disease, and it was a simple enough matter to tell red from blue. With mild chagrin he saw that his astonishment at Naldjorpa's diagnostic skill had been the result merely of ignorance. It was not long before younger *chelas* were seeking him out, calling him "Sahib Doctor" in jest, allowing him to lay hands on them, to drive out demons he himself could not name.

"Do you know what the Harvard medical faculty would say about this?" he asked Tobsan one day.

"Superstitious nonsense," his friend proclaimed, mimicking professional stuffiness so adroitly that Jed snorted in approval.

"And worse," he grinned. "Deviltry, probably. Exorcism is not much in favor there."

"Why is it," asked Tobsan, "that learned people in your country think that learned people everywhere else are merely witchdoctors?"

"No one has measured an aura. Hence auras do not exist. What would the West do without its provincialism?"

In many ways, indeed, he had come to hate the West.

What had he left there to draw him? Few friends, no family, memories of riches and guilt. No. There was no going back. The past year had worked that out of him, and for the first time in his young, priest-cluttered life he felt whole. Twelve months in this arid majestic wilderness, surrounded by nomads and monks, and he had begun to see light.

He wondered, aghast at yesterdays, what he had ever seen in it all. In the dances and fine clothing and jewels, in the rich food and travel and wines. In all the panoply of art and culture he had so loved, he could find not a single item of interest. Those long evenings over port, Bach on the victrola and Jenny's arm in his arm—what had it been for?

His country, he had come to see, was a pool of various vices. Seething with chatter and money, it had, for the price of a first-class ride, sold out its birthright, its dignity, and its pride. Nothing remained there but the dollar. No love or sympathy, not fear or courage or hope, but only the incessant twitching after gold, the endless, mounting fever to own and control the world. In place of art there was news; in place of affection, courtesy; in place of honor, a code; in place of duty, rules; and in place of courage, bravado. There was nothing in all the new building and telephones and cheering that could hold a candle to the elementary goodness of these people of the mountains.

His most vehement denunciation he reserved for the Church. If America was the daughter of the West, then Christianity was its handmaiden; all the wickedness, all the idiocy of the West's chosen way could be traced to its fantastic pursuit of the cross.

The arrogance of Christians amazed him. For a year he had wandered in this bleakest part of the world, seeking solace, seeking understanding, seeking an answer to the central unavoidable question. And everywhere he had been met with humility. Everywhere people were sympathetic, understanding, as if the spiritual journey of a young expatriate were not merely his own concern but a matter, if they could help, for all to lend a hand. Yet: they did not know either. They imagined reincarnation, they imagined demons, they imagined . . . but smiles, too, greeted him. From the highest like Naldjorpa to the lowest smith in town, smiles told him the one consolation no Christian could afford to give:

We do not know either.

That simple admission of fallibility was proof to Jed

that, whatever their social inequities, whatever their animistic dreams, the Tibetans were on to something that had not been acknowledged in the West since Constantine saw the cross. A simple people, living well, living every day with death, and having the courage not to turn aside.

Not so the West. There the notion of death, of an ending, was so abhorrent that the elaborate apparatus of the Christian afterlife had had to be invented to make the notion of mortality palatable. That was a crime against nature, a crime he could not forgive.

He was not sure which enraged him more: the morbidity of the design, or the smugness of the application. It had not been enough that the entire conception was suited only to a people who already hated its life, who would trade any earthly delight for the hope of a reward somewhere, anywhere, else. Generations of prelates had compounded this despite with another: despite for their flocks themselves. Nietzsche had been right: a sheep's religion it was. Not only had the Church announced that mortal life was hardly worth living, but it had gone the deception one further, by announcing that henceforth all remedy to the general unhappiness would proceed from a single source.

Not content to hypnotize its own people, the Church must distribute the malady worldwide. Not content with destroying all possibility of enlightenment for the "civilized" fraction of earth, outward and beyond it must go: even to the ends of the globe, even to the most isolated, ignorant pockets of heathenism; and there too plant the disease.

He had been thirteen, perhaps, when first he read of the French explorers and their consorts the missionaries. Cartier, Marquette and Joliet, La Salle. For God and for gold. Where was the snowgold now? Where were those dreams now? He remembered awe and unbounded admiration at the tales of those stolid Jesuit travelers, wood crosses round their necks, the Bible in their pouch, that fierce unregenerate indignation in their breasts as they sallied forth against the forces of darkness and despair. What a shabby lie it seemed now! For he had seen the priests at work, had felt himself the lashing of their tongues, and he knew: No country converted to the cross could hope for more than despair. Despair was their stock in trade.

Jed would have none of it. Once he had lit a single flame, in the hope that it would bring his mother back. There had been no news from the other side. Silence, as always. But now he did not care. Here, staunch against false hope, here in Tibet, he was strong.

It was in this mood of disgusted elevation that he first heard, from Tobsan, that strangers, a white man and two porters, had been sighted on the road from Nepal.

CHAPTER 9

JUDGMENTS

Jed could not say when he knew for certain that the figure approaching was Will. High noon it was. He and Tobsan had taken advantage of the general excitement that the arrival of the Westerner's party had caused to remove themselves from their regular duties and make their way to a secluded wall, there to observe, undisturbed by the chatter of younger monks, the descent of the three into the valley. They knew this infraction of monastic discipline would bring a caning, but no new white face had been seen in Lhasa since Jed's own arrival six months earlier, and the chance of witnessing such a novelty was not to be missed merely for the sake of a few bruises.

No shadows attended the trio as they strode silently down the riverbed into town. Near the city gates a crowd had gathered, and above their shifting heads Jed could make out the red and white banners of the Tashi Lama, principal secular authority of the kingdom: his retinue, officially garbed in amber and gold, milled warily about him, prepared to exert the influence of their six-foot hardwood staffs on the person of any of the travellers deemed unworthy of entrance into the holy city.

"A man," said Tobsan, "and two women."

That shambling, erect carriage, as though the figure

were striding, Deadwater Dick, into a showdown. The hand pulling at his chin. The sandy top, cropped military fashion. A type, perhaps, Jed thought; and yet, no, it could be no one else but Will.

He squinted hard, placing a hand above the full, even brows so that he looked the part of a nearsighted Indian scout straining to identify brass buttons, blue twill.

"I know him, Tobsan."

His friend smiled, clapped an easy hand around his shoulders. "And you thought they had given you up."

The crowd parted. From its midst a lean figure in the scarlet robes of the high lamas came out to meet the arrivals. Behind him the retinue waited.

"Will they let them in?"

Jed's voice was anxious, yet he could not say his pleasure in Will's coming was unmixed. Will was of the West, and so suspect. Eager as the young man may have been for news, for renewal of bonds, he considered himself now, however prematurely, a Tibetan, and so he half expected the party to be turned back and himself to accept the event with firm, if grating, equanimity. There was, indeed, a level of his being which wanted the trio turned around.

"Perhaps," said Tobsan. "Who is it, then?"

"I have known him," he replied, "since we were children. I owe him, even if he had not risked himself to come here, more than I can say. And yet . . ."

The hand gripped, comforting. "It hurts, yes? That, somewhere deep, you do not wish to see him?"

"I guess I've not been here long enough for that to go. Yes, it does hurt. He was my best friend, before you. That's not easily put aside. What are their chances, do you think?"

"He speaks no Tibetan?"

"Wouldn't hear of it, I should think."

"Well, then: we had better be down. They will be coming for us soon."

"For us?"

"The Capuchins are gone," he said quietly, "and the soldiers, so goes the prophecy, are not due for another six years. If the lamas wish to know his business, it is only us who can translate for them."

To let Will in: that only he could say. Irony, Jed mused, was no surprise here, but a way of life.

They watched the crowd sway, the trio held where it was, surrounded by the constabulary, as a runner made his way back down the river, bore north, jogged through the pleasant August heat up the hill to the Potala. "We should go down, now. It won't do for them to find us here when we're wanted."

Jed nodded. They descended the stone stairs, made their way as inconspicuously as possible into the back of the dimly lit dining hall, where their fellows were just now completing the meal which their curiosity had lost them, and sat.

It was not until late afternoon that the messenger had gone through the protocol on the other hill, made his way down and across the valley and up this side, and delivered to the Chakpori abbot the Dalai Lama's official request that Tobsan and Jed be excused from their duties for the remainder of the day. A perfunctory approval, and the two were hustled off, tan robes streaming behind them, to meet the travellers from the West.

Summer was nearly gone. The valley floor, a kaleidoscope of purples and greens only a few weeks before, was beginning to show the first signs of exhaustion; already the green of the foothills was turning, and the breezes that coursed down the slopes of the crystal highlands were now sharp with the suggestion of winter. If the lamas should decide he might not stay, thought Jed, they would just make it back across the passes in time.

"Why," he asked Tobsan, "all this fuss, when there was nothing at all for me?"

"It is you, and not he," answered his friend, "that are the exception. We are jealous of our land. That is because of our history. Foreigners have seldom brought anything but pain, and so the lamas are cautious."

Fifty yards away, up a gentle rise, Will Detroit peered at the approaching figures. The robes had him stymied, but something in the gait of the taller figure, some eccentric bounce to the step, was familiar. He rose from the rock where he had been waiting for the past three hours and began to walk down the rise. He had got ten feet when crossed staves blocked his way. But yes, yes, it was. A hand on Kamala's shoulder, a glance of recognition and thanks. They looked with amusement at the stiff sahib they had brought through the mountains, now transformed, by agencies unknown, into a gleeful, boyish clown. He laughed loud, clapped hands.

"Well, Dey, I'll be damned!"

Jed's head up, ears wondering, of knowing, yes: from what millions of leagues he had come, to what code of honor bound, he did not know. He knew only that here, a sprint away, was one he had played with young: cowboys and Indians, the sun on Sheep Meadow, summers at the Cape. Their eyes together, the curiosity and awe and delight of the one locking with the relief and the wan, nostalgic pride of the other; here, for an instant in the crisp Himalayan dusk, the two were ten again.

Breaking from Tobsan, breaking thoughtless, free of time, Jed ran toward his friend. Will started running toward him too, the staves lifted at an unseen command, and the two hit, hard, funny, like bumping cars in this ancient valley.

"Welcome," said Jed, "to Tibet."

Then back, and surprise met, voiced: "What the hell is that getup anyway?"

"And what the hell," Jed winked back, "is yours?"

The two old friends backed off, appraising, holding each other at arms' length, mutually aghast. Around them the Tashi Lama's retinue leaned expectant on their sticks. There was no doubt, after their greeting, that Will would be allowed entrance into the city: the Tibetans' natural courtesy could not turn away one who had been so heartily welcomed by one of their own monks, no matter how marginal an allegiance that monk might profess to the nation. How long they would let him stay, however, remained to be seen. Murmurings near, Jed in his pleasure oblivious. Then:

"Tashi would know your business."

The voice was Tobsan's. Will, not fully reconciled to the exotic garb of the friend he had last seen in tweeds, looked up, caught the steady, friendly gaze of the young Mongol.

Looking at Jed, his enthusiasm aflame, Will began with ingenuous indignation. "What is this anyway? Tell these fellows to put down those sticks a moment. Haven't seen you in Lord knows how long, I'm dusty and tired . . ."

"All of Tibet apologizes for your inconvenience, Will," smiled Jed. "But these fellows, as you say, are the Praetorian guard here. They will permit you access to this land only after knowing the nature of your mission."

"My mission! Well, by dammit, you know my mission well enough! I've come to take you home."

Jed looked fondly, radiant, at his friend, met his gaze briefly, and spoke over his shoulder. "Tell them, Tobsan, that our friend has come to pay his respects to a holy place and to visit for a time with me, the companion of his childhood."

153

"Sententious enough, yes," Tobsan muttered, and translated the speech.

"For a time . . ." Will's face darkened briefly, but the cloud passed when the lama raised a hand in salute and welcomed him officially into the kingdom. Instantly a dozen hands were at the travelers' call, snatching up packs, extended in greeting, clapping in rhythmic welcome. Down into the valley they moved, Tobsan ahead with the guards, Will and Jed arm in arm, a year and a century to span.

"You didn't mean that, did you, Jed? What you said about my visiting . . . for a time?"

"How was your journey, Will? I'm proud as hell you came."

"The journey? Oh, great. No problem. I have to get on you some time about that friend of yours Scarfer. Did you really give him your watch?"

A quick slice of annoyance twisted Jed's features. Then: "He would accept nothing else. And we had to get over the mountains."

"But your father's watch, Jed! I hate to see something you both love in the hands of that scoundrel."

"It was only a watch, Will. It means very little here. Your porters were satisfactory?"

"Fine," Will nodded. "I thought I might be getting a pig in a poke with these gals here, but I was wrong, wrong as can be. I was afraid they'd be useless in a jam, you see, but the little one, Kamala there, she was as good as gold, good as gold. Damn near got done in by a leopard last week, but she put a slug right between his eyes. I tell you, she sure knows how to handle a carbine. Took them along for bandits, see, but we never did spot any. Where the hell have you been anyway? Where's your father?"

"My father. Yes. Your bandits. I'm glad you avoided them. We . . . were not so lucky."

Will's exuberance turned to hushed expectation.

"What happened?" he asked slowly.

Jed breathed once deep, exhaled gradually, as if to expel the memory one more time.

"It seems a long time ago. Not much to tell, really. They were after money, rings, jewelry. He didn't feel any pain."

Acid bit the corners of the traveler's mouth. A firm, lean hand grasped, squeezed Jed's shoulder.

"God damn wilderness!" he spat.

They gave him a week. It would be, he thought, plenty of time to wean Jed away from the exotica that had, in this last lost year, gotten such a hold on his mind. Aware as Will had been of Jed's interest in the East, even before the expedition, he had not been prepared for such a total conversion as his friend's announcement of his intention to stay suggested. And generous of heart as he was, he could not help feeling a little resentful of the thoroughness and rapidity with which this mysterious land had seized his former companion's affection and distorted, so it seemed, his common sense.

One would not have thought that a single year here could have changed him so much. Only last Thanksgiving, he recalled with some annoyance, the two of them had spent the better part of an afternoon lounging in Holmohr's den, devouring cognac and arguing about Bryan and free silver. Now, a bare year later, Jed was decked out in robes, sworn off anything stronger than tea, and not in the least interested in politics. Why, he had appeared entirely unaffected by the news that McKinley had won!

What in hell was he doing here in the first place? He longed for the clean, predictable melodies of his childhood: the music of Haydn and Bach. Here they had no such masters. Will's ears hungered for a single line of song he could cling to, a single mounting harmony that would captivate him, trap him boundless and blessed, as did the Messiah oratorio, into that curious refreshing rapture that great Art always gave him. There was always something missing here. Nothing really satisfied. Too much mist, as his father would say.

They had magnificent mountains, yes, and the air was bracing, and he could see why Jed would want to spend time here. But a lifetime, my God! A lifetime among a people infested with lice, a people whose very existence refuted Progress—no, that was too much! Will loved his friend, but despaired of ever being able to comprehend the mistiness of his motives, of his hates and loves and designs.

He was a simple man, in fact. He gave as much as he was worth, and he expected the same, whether this applied to money, hope, or love. He was also unsubtly Western, and so more confused than Jed about the crisis they were living through. In all his trekking across deserts, in all his fearful wonder whether his friend was still alive, in all his bewildered journey of mercy through these valleys of perdition, the one thing that never occurred to Will was that Jed would refuse to come home. It seemed intemperate, absurd.

He had seen his friend on these larks before. There had been the vegetable diet when he was fourteen, the fling with yoga some years later, and then, at Harvard, the obsession with what he had called "cosmic"—as opposed to "pragmatic"—philosophies. But that was done. Will had not expected a renascence of those adolescent reveries now that Jed was past age, a man about to inherit a fortune and take his place in society. It was unseemly, unbecoming to a person of his standing.

His father, he knew, would blame Harvard, that hotbed of "free-thinkers and bohemians." Will was subtler. Perhaps Cambridge had sown the seeds of discontent, but it had been the journey, this mad jaunt through lands to which his mind was simply not properly attuned, that had set Jed off on his vaporous musings. Tobsan, no doubt, had had a part in it. Will fought down the ungenerous impulse to blame the foreigner for Jed's fall, dimly conscious he was not willing to pit himself against the Tibetan in a race for their friend's favors. There was more here at stake than personality.

The journey, yes, had done it. John Pierre had been dead for six months. With Jed still in crepe for his mother. It was no wonder his mind had come out of it twisted.

And yet he was not crazed. Or seemed not, anyway. Lucid as ever, and as funny. The old sparks there, sure enough: Will could not say that, whatever the eccentricity of his path, his friend had suffered in either acumen or humor by his ordeal. Sharp he was still, and more. Something more there was to him now: some hint of an unusual stolidity, a new conviction. That irony that had always distinguished Jed's manner of speech, that constant suggestion that, whatever he held, its opposite laughed beneath—that was absent now. The crudity of his new creed aside, Will could not deny that Jed, for the first time since he could remember, had accepted it whole.

And that bothered him. It suggested foul play, ungentlemanly conduct on the part of Jed's Tibetan hosts. How but through devious methods could they have so rapidly transformed an alert, questioning mind into a mass of Oriental gibberish?

Will was not complicated by this place. These months among the wastes of the East had given him little more than an anxious, sensitive tourist's appreciation of its soul. Calcutta, yes, had affected him deeply, and Kathmandu as well. Whatever sophisticated resignation to social evil he had picked up at the hands of William Graham Sumner and the other social Darwinists, his heart was finally too wide, his stomach too easily turned, for him to be able to ignore the misery of this half of the earth. His resolve to do something to alleviate the poverty here was heartfelt and direct: he would do whatever he could, upon his return to New York.

But that was surface. It took little insight to see that Asia in 1897 was a mess. The broader, murkier depths of the place had escaped him, and he them. The *Gita,* the *Upanishads,* all that panoply of high-minded mistiness that Jed took so to heart—it had never seized his curiosity or rattled him into despair. Perhaps if he had seen his father killed, had nearly frozen to death himself, things would have been different. In the event he had but a cursory acquaintance with Jed's philosophical confusions.

At the age of twenty-one, Will Detroit was still a believing Christian, and his belief, erratic as may have been his practice of it, made it impossible for him to see Jed's transformation as anything but accidental, mysterious—and reversible. He sought the answer for their common dilemma in the rationalist's chimera: there must be a single reason, clear if elusive, why Jed had decided to stay.

For this he had two choices.

First he had thought it was the gold. The metal that had killed his father: was it not fitting that the son should continue the quest, should secure the grail for which such a heavy price had already been paid? Not for Holmohr now, but for himself alone. And not for the value of the thing, either, but for something less substantial, less physically substantial anyway: glamour, perhaps, or pride.

But no. Jed was romantic enough for that, but he was not foolish. A year of his life, maybe, he would spend tracing the spoor of Holmohr's dream; but more than that, no. Not Jed, not for a symbol.

His father, then. It all came back to his father. The old man had died, in what circumstances only Jed himself knew, and now it was up to the son to make sure that debts were paid. A man kills your father, you are obliged. Obliged to stay even in this hypnotic desolation, until the killer is found, tried, hanged. Yes. What else, finally, could it be? Jed, his friend concluded, would remain in Tibet until the bandit was dead and his father avenged.

A grim smile passed his lips. He was satisfied, and more, with the explanation. It was, after all, the decent thing to do. He could not hold it against him.

And yet, somehow, a way must be found out of the morass. The chances that even another year would result in the capture and conviction of the bandit were remote; the chances this could be accomplished in time to get the two of them back to New York this year were probably infinitesimal. What could a friend do? Heavily Will felt the obligations of friendship, and heavier still those of fraternity. He had, after all, a dual responsibility here, for he had come not only on Jed's own behalf, but on Jenny's.

To have come all this way, and to fail! What little satisfaction he felt came from the fact that he knew the reason for the impasse. It lifted a burden from his clean, uncluttered mind to accept the second explanation: to avenge a parricide, yes, that was something even his own father would understand. Will rested easier now. What reason had explained, reason could resolve. He would sleep on it. In the morning he would see Jed again. In a week, God willing, they would be off.

In the end it was decided for them. The lamas had allotted Jed a day in the town to trade counsel with his past, to gather and finish the unknit threads of whatever it was he shared with Will Detroit.

They met at noon, just off the bazaar, Jed in his robes, Will looking uncomfortable in the linen tunic and trousers that were unofficial regulation gear for a sahib in this climate. The day was mild for September, and Will had constant resort to the handkerchief protruding from his breast pocket. Sweat was ever his nemesis.

They strolled through Lhasa's chaos, chatting of home, trading names of friends, striving not to recognize how radically their paths had diverged in the past year. In the end it was decided for them.

Rumbles of the crowd: lost syllables, a phrase of anger or glee, the sense of something about to happen. Will and Jed moved closer to the mass, craning necks with little effort over the shorter Tibetans, seeking the cause of the noise.

"What is it?" Jed asked a young man straining toward the center of the commotion.

He uttered a single Tibetan word. Death was no stranger here: it no longer struck Jed as surprising that within his still meager Tibetan vocabulary should be found the word for "execution." Calmly he explained this to Will.

Over the heads of the curious the two Americans made out the scene. Retinue of the Tashi Lama, staves now aside, and among them, bound, two men. One slender, gangly, the other stocky, muscled, his head a mass of thick black hair. Jed squinted, wonder rising:

something in the neck, the swagger of short bones, alerted him.

Fat, and sat his horse well.

Not now.

But yes, it was the one. It was him, silent, a stone: Blacktooth.

"Not long on mercy here, are they?" Will's picque of sentiment drifted in and out of his hearing. "They'd be dead in an hour anyway the way they've tied those bonds."

The judgment had already been given. What crime the two had committed Jed had no way of knowing: what wayward walker had come victim to their knives, what riches wrested, blood spilled—of this he was as ignorant as Will.

Creaking corners of his mouth, a hand raised, the tan robes falling to the elbow, and no sound. Around him the crowd a single chant for vengeance.

Justice was swift here. For such and such offense against the peace of his most holy presence Thubten Gyatso, the thirteenth Dalai Lama, you have been found guilty and are hereby condemned to death. Deafening shouts, and the end.

The scene was ten yards away; it might have been ten miles. Within the chanting of the crowd Jed could make out nothing intelligible. Blood was what they wanted, the questions had been sealed. His mouth open, the back of his throat locked, he screamed with them, knowing dimly there was beyond this no expectation of understanding or help for pain, but justice alone, grim and final.

They picked the two up, lifting them high enough so that even on the edges of the crowd where Will and Jed stood the defiant black mouth might be seen. No cries from either of them, no hint that mercy was expected. A glance of wild eyes Jed caught, and then—gone.

161

They dragged the bandits to a cliffside. Jed followed dumbly, cheers caught in the throat, Will's wonder companion to his confusion. Bouncing, shuffling with the townspeople, they came to within a handsthrow of the victims and stopped, enjoying the false placidity of the suddenly subdued mob. Then, abruptly, the Tashi Lama drew out a long sunstruck blade, raised it ceremonially so that it glinted in the sun. The crowd surged.

Not like this, not like this.

The end was not elaborate. No speeches, no farewells, no prayers. Sanctity here resided not in the body but in the spirit, and time would not be wasted eulogizing the shortcomings of two nameless outlaws. For an instant Jed's stomach dipped, pity for the indignity of these lives bringing salt to his clean Cartesian eyes. Then, breaking, he was one with the crowd, one voice hard for revenge. The blade aloft, and a single gasping sound.

But in that moment . . .

In that second before the blade severed the black-toothed head from the shoulders, the head rose to scan the cheering crowd, and a twist of mirth transfixed the features. It was Kidd on the gallows, defiant to the last.

His smile ranged the throng, locked on Jed.

In that last instant, he could not be mistaken. The bandit's expression spoke neither of hatred nor of pride. There was an elemental transparency to the eyes, which evoked in Jed, against all his efforts to resist it, a recollection of the way he had felt at the base of Dhaulagiri seconds before Naldjorpa arrived.

For a few moments the two stared at each other, while Jed savored the eccentricity of the feeling, the sharpness of knowing that, beyond all justice or mercy, he and his father's killer were one.

Briefly the black eyes danced, and Jed bowed in

recognition. In those culprit eyes, the secret he had lost lived again. In that last moment, he looked, seeking, hoping, thankful to the one man he should hate without reservation for a second chance at the truth.

The blade a silver banner above. The bandit's eyes held Jed's. Not apology or pleading for forgiveness; not defiance or laughter or fear; but something far more deeply intermingled with the young man's own sorry history, something to say, beyond all the gaps of breeding and goldlust and age: we are lost, or saved, together.

Shaking, falling, the blade.

Dumb still, his eyes watered for his father or himself or the killer of them both, he did not know. Beyond his control, Jed's arm raised in salute. The executioner's arm went up a moment later. The bandit grinned once, dropped his head, and waited.

The blade fell. The head rolled into the dirt. It was done.

CHAPTER 10

ALONE

"But dammit, Jed, there's no reason to stay now!"

To Will it could not have been clearer. The execution of the bandit had removed any doubt that Jed's purpose in this godforsaken land was at an end. The gold, he knew, could not still hold his friend's mind. "The baron should find his own booty," he had told him yesterday. As for the dubious attractions of monastic life, well, a brisk sea journey and the first sight of the Statue of Liberty would set that to rights.

Revenge, he was convinced, had been the sole reason Jed had been reluctant to leave Tibet; now that the state had, as it were, performed the necessary ablutions for him, his way was open as day. What quirk of orneriness or sardonic wit compelled him now to keep up this charade, this exotic shadow play among barbarians?

"It just makes no sense. None at all. The bastard has met his due. Why on earth would you want to stay on here?"

Jed's voice was low. He pressed his eyes lightly together, sniffed the first strains of winter through cedar. "Who knows?" he murmured.

"Jed . . ." The tone was exasperated, but short of venom. "If we leave now, we can be in London by Christmas. Plum pudding, caroling, walks on the Strand. It'll be smashing fun. Remember that pudgy doorman at the Dorchester? His tales of Gordon and the Sudan? I bet you he's still there. And Sothebys, Jed! We could take on some of these banners—what d'you call them, *tankas?* I bet Father's never seen one of them. Holmohr would love it . . . he can't tell gold from brass, he's getting so old now. Bring him a bauble, he'll never know the difference . . ."

"It's not the gold, Will."

He stopped short. He was aware that his enthusiasm was inappropriate. What, though? What could he be thinking of?

"If we don't leave now, it's up for another year. We can't get over the passes come November." Somber he was, falling quiet. "What's to hold you here, Jed?"

The October sun was high. They were sitting on a wall halfway up the slope of Chakpori, ringed by cedar trees. Jed had been released again from his duties so that he might confront this eager Westerner who, little more than a year before, he had called his closest friend. Around them the Himalayas shone. Jed laid a hand on Will's wrist. "The mountains, perhaps," he whispered.

Guarding against misunderstanding: "I'm trying, Will. Trying to speak frankly. We've not seen each other for so long. Remember that summer at Newport when Jenny stayed out all night at the Van Damms? You were livid. Your mother—"

"Jenny . . . yes."

Their eyes met, locked as if they were fourteen, drifted indolent toward the mountains. "What the hell am I going to tell *her,* damn you?"

Jed did not know this man. No longer. Ten years they had loved one another, as boys and rivals and young men. One year had taken them apart. Deaths. Three deaths had done it, and now? What could he tell him?

He looked once, close, at the aristocratic profile, the

clean blue eyes gazing in mute confusion over the valley of the Brahmaputra. What could he say to him? That far from releasing him from his quest, the death of the bandit had only confirmed what he had already known for some time: that he must stay in Tibet. Could he explain how, in that last fearless second before the head left the body, the parricide had met his gaze, thrown up a challenge, demanded of the boy something that even his own wrangling with Dhaulagiri had not prepared him for? No: these were not things he would understand.

Jenny would, though, and for that Jed was thankful. The hand squeezed the wrist. "Tell her I have found something worth doubting," he said.

He had meant to be kind, but it did not come out so. The blue eyes squeezed back, bitter, fighting salt, and the thin mouth crackled.

"What the hell are you talking about?"

"She'll understand," he said absently. Then, softer: "Will, I don't like this either. Don't you think I've missed you, and her, and home? But there's something here for me. I can't explain it yet, but it's here. It's not my choice. I cannot leave this place."

Anger and concern bridled together. "They're not locking you up?"

The hand loosened. "No. Nothing like that. I mean that there are questions. Questions about my life. I have been trying to answer them since my mother died. I cannot answer them in New York."

"And here?" The sweep of the manicured hand, the curl of mouth, suggested limited awe, a sense of wonder not quite rich enough to overcome the young man's patrician repugnance at a country whose magic had stolen his best friend's mind and placed him, babbling, in robes.

"Perhaps," Jed nodded.

"What questions?"

He would try to say it once. Simply as he could, so that he would not have later to chide himself with failure to have appreciated the suffering of another, failure to throw the line. At least that. He spoke slowly.

"I am not the person you knew. My father is not the only one who has died. I have died too. This is not a game, Will. I don't understand what has happened to me, God knows I don't; but I'll be damned if I'll go back to New York without giving it a good try to find out. I have not told you much about the killing. I have not told you about what came after. What happened then means I cannot go back, not now, maybe not ever. I came"—he measured his words slowly, pressing thumb and forefinger together for emphasis—"that close to being dead myself. I swear to you, sometimes I don't know whether I made it through or not."

"Oh, for God's sakes, Jed—"

"You do not know!"

The sharpness of the response surprised them both. "I'm sorry, Will. But you don't. Nor do I. At one point, I knew I was done for. No doubt left. Nothing. I was dead, and that was all there was to it. I saw things then that . . ."

He trailed off. Will turned.

"What things?"

For a moment the two were silent. Somewhere off, gongs. It was time, almost, for meditation. Jed shifted, arranged the folds of tan about him. It irritated him that the intrusion should come at just this point, and he chuckled at the appropriateness. Shrugging, he continued.

"Not . . . God, I guess. No. Visions, we would call them, maybe. Another kind of world. Just as real, just as alive as this one, but . . ."

He laughed aloud completing the thought: ". . . but dead."

The comradely arm now Will's. "Look, Jed," he worked out slowly, "I know you've been through a hell of a lot. It must have been awful for you these past months, not knowing, not hearing anything—it was for us, I know. But that's all over now. You're here, I'm here, we're both of us alive and well, thank God. And you've just got to get back on the track, get your life moving again."

The hint of annoyance, a wrinkle at the eyes. "It is moving, Will. On a different track, perhaps, but moving nonetheless."

"All right, all right, I just mean that, well, dammit, you know what I mean! You can't go on wondering all your life about whether you're really here or not. We both damn well know you're here. You made it! Thank God, and let's get on with it! All that Bishop Berkeley stuff gives me a pain in the neck. Is what I see *really* what I see? Really, Jed, that's all right for college, but we're men now, we've got responsibilities, things to do. Kick a rock, for goodness's sakes."

A grin in spite of himself. Will had always had a knack of making him smile. "I've tried that one, Will."

"Well, then, what's to do here? There's nothing here but mountains and monks. You . . . you're fit for more than this, Jed."

"More?"

"Goddammit, there's a world for the taking out there! New York! You should see it now, Jed! You wouldn't believe the parties! The Astors gave a ball last season that—oh, well, I don't suppose you want to hear about that. But hell! There's a world!"

He flung his arm out again, and Jed was struck by the contrast between the way Naldjorpa and this genial young American presented him the Himalayas. "This is fine, sure. Fine. But you don't belong here. You belong with your own people. You were born to it. These folks here . . . well, they're very nice, but . . . what kind of life is this? You don't surely"—his voice dropped, hints of horror, miscomprehension—"intend to spend your *whole life* here?"

"I had thought eventually," Jed replied softly, "to go to India."

Will was silent. The two watched the sun. Gongs again. Ten minutes more, they both knew, and Jed would be off, and Will would go for the porters. It must not end like this.

"I've been to India. It's horrible. I'd like to . . . help, send something. But *live* there? I don't understand what you think you can gain by leaving us. What is here for you?"

"Leaving you? I am not leaving you, Will. We have grown in different ways. Neither of us could help that. You are content in New York, I am not. What is so difficult—"

"How on earth can you know if you don't even *try*? Don't you think you owe us that? Come back for a month, a week. Look around. You'll forget this, this chanting, this weather, the dirt—God, Jed, this is no part of you!"

This, then, his oldest friend. *And all coherence gone.* Glumly Jed noted the handkerchief, the goatee he had affected while at Yale and kept, as a memento of those bright years, ever since.

"My way," he said, salt rising, "cannot be yours."

"You are worth," Will said deliberately, "ten million dollars."

"Ten *million?*"

It would feed Nepal for a year.

Will nodded. "What will you do with that? Do you have no conception of the responsibility that your

169

wealth entails? Do you have no concern how it should be spent?"

"It is not my wealth. It is my father's wealth, and Holmohr's. It has not, I am sad to admit, eased my mind. You may do with it what you want."

"What *I* want? Who am I? This is your birthright, Jed! Does it mean nothing to you? Your family is old, respected; all of New York knows your name. Will you throw all of that over for a lark?"

He would not understand. Finally, irretrievably, Will was of his time and his place. Jed saw that now, accepted it with the fond sorrow of a past necessarily denied, and at last he knew what little he could do to link hands with this quivering memory.

"I trust you, Will," he said simply. "Your love I trust, and your judgment. The money I leave in your hands. I am not so flippant to demand it be distributed among the poor, although perhaps that would be best. You decide. With all due love for you, for Jenny, for what we have shared, I wash my hands of that. It was gold that killed my father. It will not be gold that kills me. You decide."

"That's it, then? I get on my hobby horse and trek back to Calcutta, you stay here with the incense. That part of your life is over. God, Jed, how bitter you make me feel!"

Jed, silent, twitched. A few times he had seen this uncrooked man weep. His heart moved out, sought response, and there was none. It had gone beyond history now, though Will would not see it so. There was a larger question now, and no amount of recrimination over opportunities lost, loves denied, could counter the central fact: his life now, for better or worse, was in Tibet. The hand barely reached to the shoulder and Will was stiff, retracted.

170

"If ever you change your mind . . . well—you know where we are."

And gone. Through a salt fog Jed watched the lean form retreat, wind down the stone steps toward the plain and the porters and home.

A third time the gongs, and he rose.

Night. The last link gone, Jed contemplated where his days had brought him.

Will had been gone since sunrise. It was fall now: a year, almost, since the crime. A year to go, if he were lucky, before Will would be back in New York. What chaos, unseen, unplanned, had interrupted the placid course of his life in these bitter twelve months. He felt it now deeper, more astringently even, than he had felt it that distant day in the shadow of Dhaulagiri: how, the lofty schemes of the Holmohrs and Detroits notwithstanding, it was the unexpected that generally proved momentous.

In his case a golden medallion, the chance appearance of a wandering anchorite, the swift justice of the Tibetan state, had conspired to secure his place here, *chela* among aliens, outcast irrecoverably from his own.

Will's departure had deepened the weather, made fully, finally clear to him how completely he had cut himself off from his past. True, he had resolved long before last week to remain as long as necessary— "until I find the gold," he recalled smiling—but it was only the unexpected arrival of his friend that had given that resolution teeth, made it a thing not of fancy, however fervent, but of pointed, unshakable conviction.

Night. His small cell. A few books, the begging bowl, candles. This, now, was his life. If his need before had been heartfelt, now it was more than need. He had sacrificed for this now; it would not be easily put aside.

He began to see Will's coming and rapid going as a

test met and won. But no: there was not winning and losing here. That was to be gone beyond. A test nonetheless. Yes: it was done, now, there was no going back. He experienced now, the candles casting eeriness about him, a sense of curious exhilaration, quick despair. It was cooler than the mountains. That had been empty, the end. He felt now, on the contrary, that he had all too much to live for, and was struck by the anomalous sparseness of this life to which he was now granting allegiance. Gone the last way back, the single half-expected rescue; now truly he was on his own.

He delighted in the incomparable lightness of the man with nothing to his name.

Names would go as well. He, the last of his line, had surrendered that dubious dignity along with the title to his estate, membership in the Century Club, the hand of Jennifer Detroit. Nothing was left him now, and the recognition that he had consciously, with full if shadowed intent, brought this situation of poverty on himself cheered him in a manner he had not been cheered since the first fine flushes, somewhere around nineteen, of undeniable apostasy.

To be abandoned, orphaned and disowned, was one thing; to invite privation, to embrace isolation as a positive aid to understanding rather than as a merciless heaven's fillip: this gave, he felt, freedom. For the first time in his life he understood the power of penury, the inestimable dignity of a deliberately limited existence.

Time, for a time, was held. He felt, the shadows a tomb or a dawn, he could justify to himself—himself. If this room were all he would ever know, why that would be a burden, finally, lighter than the "responsibilities" Will was fond of. He could nod a yes, a hearty one even, to such simpleness.

A glimmer on the edges of his thought. No thinking

more, no doubleness, but only this pale grey stonewall, the ice cave again, around him in a hard embrace, until at any next second, the end.

All right. He breathed deeply, incense ravaging the nostrils, and coughed, smiled at the bleakness of the revelation, the humor of physical infirmity. As if, having made it off the mountain, he could ever have thought the game was up and he with the prize.

There are no winners in this game.

He was moving now, he realized with a pale, creeping pleasure, into a period of negatives. Goodbye to Will meant not only a choice against plutocracy, but a drift, beyond his control, into everything.

Into, in the final reckoning, nothing.

And yet this was not despair. No, he was lifted, challenged, thrilled by it! The excitement of life on the edge: nothing before in his life had come near to the calm expansiveness he now felt as he considered that, very probably, he would never again leave these mountains. Two years, even a year ago, he would have, like Will, considered that immurement; now it was possibility.

To have nothing, finally, was to have it all.

Beyond this plateau? He was content to imagine it ending here. He placed his hands behind his head and grinned idiotically.

"Are you here, then?"

The voice might have been his own, but it was Tobsan's. Behind him his friend was grinning also.

"It is time for you to go."

The thin Mongolian face was a beam of recognition, as if Tobsan had known what depths of acceptance Jed had attained, as if he had timed his arrival to catch his friend at just the moment before it all sank in. A shred of annoyance passed.

"Go?" he asked.

"Come," he said simply. "It is your time."

Jed followed. The hunger within, the hunger of mind, urged sandaled steps down from the *chelas'* level, down eight levels more until the two stood before a massive wooden door, deep, Jed calculated, within the mountain on which the monastery was built. Tobsan stopped, turned, and a noncommittal smile flickered the thin lips.

"Beyond this door there is a corridor. At the end of the corridor, you will find, perhaps, an answer. Go now, and I will see you tomorrow. Remember one thing. It is only when you have surrendered your hunger that you find food."

He was gone.

Jed listened to his steps echo up the stone, then tried the door. It swung inward with a juicy creaking of hinges. Before him was a narrow stone stair lit by torches. He entered, descended. At the bottom of the stair was another door. He pushed one, two, and it opened.

Light dazzled, soundless and brilliant. A single, uniform sheet of white rushed out of the earth, reached to him, offered hands of flame. He was not afraid. Snow-gold, he muttered, and laughed.

For before him was the gold.

As a single icon it shone. Rings and medallions by the score, all with the brilliance of Hajib's disc. Bracelets and neckpieces, goblets and plaques and ornamental weapons, all of that inestimable, deathly pallor, the color of his hope and his decline. A hundred regents' ransoms, it filled the underground chamber with a light no earthly smith had seen. For this, legions of men would die.

He had been given it, there could be no doubt, only because he had no longer desired it. The lamas' jesting hit him well, rolled up through empty innards, tickled brains, touched the deepest of larks in a frame beyond pride and despair. Dazzled, he was, but not done.

A clear, serene comprehension lifted him beyond the smokiness of the torchlight, beyond Jethro Dey and the mountain and this glittering, dreamer's vault. He was on the plain again, and the reaper, no longer grim, was near. He could do nothing less than smile.

Behind him, a familiar air. He turned.

Naldjorpa was leaning, grinning also, on a staff. Jed's mouth moved effortlessly, a crackle of delight. It was, as he had said it would be, time. In the grey impossible eyes: snowgold.

The old man spoke softly.

"You are ready," he said, "to begin."

प्रेम